Four minutes after  he
resistance increase \ll
enemies so far h. The
commandos climbed another set of stairs. They were shot at
by another operator. The Spectre ducked and called out on the
radio, "Contact left! Contact left! Taking fire! I repeat: taking
fire!"

"Six to Two-One. Give me a SITREP. Over," responded Red
Six on the radio.

"Charlie Fox. Shit!" he yelled as the bullets sprayed over his
head. Tiny impact craters blasted into the stairwell wall adjacent to the wall the combatant was using for cover. "This is
Two-One. Small arms fire from eleven o'clock. 10 meters out."

The enemy opp stood prepared around a corner with a
5.56×45mm Rockwell SL15 rifle stock tucked firmly into his
shoulder. The terrorist wore a double reinforced armored vest,
(bullet resistant and tear resistant, not bulletproof or inde-
structible). He watched for the first visible reappearance of the
Spectre's helmet above the final step. The commando
collapsed. Blood had splattered against his shattered visor.

As the succeeding Spectres snaked up the stairwell, their
new friend underhand tossed a grenade that bounced down-
wards around the corners by their feet. The Marines dove for
what little cover they could muster in the split second. There
were worse ways to go, but not many.

TERMINAL VELOCITY

Ingram Spark ISBN #979-8-8691-3547-6

KDP ISBN #979-8-3400-4579-9

First Edition: Dec 2024

AUTHOR'S NOTE

A comprehensive glossary awaits readers at the book's end, offering clarity on key terms and concepts explored within these pages. Please consult this resource freely, as it has been designed to enhance understanding and facilitate a deeper engagement with the material presented.

The dialogue in this story is presented in modern American English. The actual idioms and words are imperfectly translated to a dialect we can understand. If in the distant future our descendants are speaking English, it will likely be far different than the words we use today.

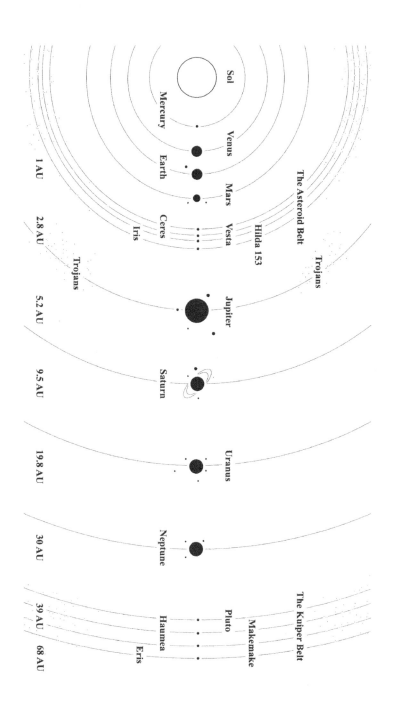

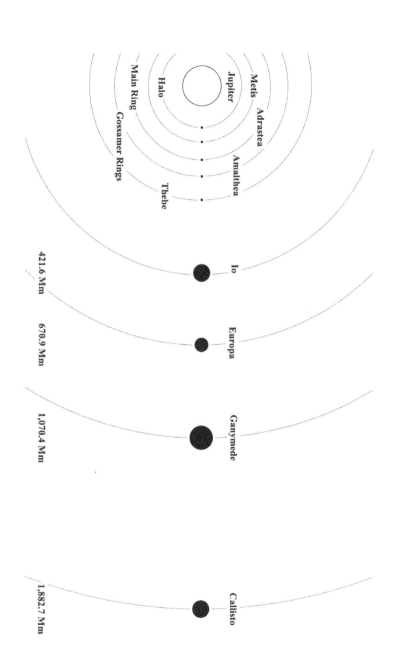

For my dogs.

TERMINAL VELOCITY

JOSEF KAINRAD

1

IT ALWAYS KILLED THE CHILDREN FIRST.

The monitor flatlined. Items stained red lay on the instrument tray: scissors, a syringe, first-aid tape, gauze bandages, and a vial of anesthetic. The medical lab was filled with rows of beds occupied by children connected to a myriad of tubes and vital monitors.

Dr. Michael Walker began checking multiple leads on the flatlined machine to ensure the absence of any anomalous electrical impulses. It was necessary for them to document every single step in the rapid destruction of human life during their experiment. As Walker worked, his colleague Dr. Jessica Mercer pressed on the sternum of the child to check for a reaction. Walker peeled open the eyelids and held up a flashlight, but the pupils remained fixed and dilated.

"Alright. I'm callin' it." Walker checked his watch and recorded, "Time of Death 0715."

This was the third one this week.

Mercer grimaced.

"Put the body on ice and move it to the autopsy facility for post-op."

"Yes ma'am," Walker replied.

The two were interrupted as another young girl gasped for breath in the faint stages of a death rattle on a bed parallel to them. The haunting sound was not exactly music to their ears.

"Euthanize that one."

Walker avoided eye contact with the child as he checked the intravenous access point for a secure connexion. For all his years of education, a secure IV site wasn't exactly his speciality. She winced. Walker injected a liberal dose of pentobarbital directly into her IV bag. The medication reached her circulatory system and she suffered cardiac arrest within 15 minutes.

The Jovian system's ruthless hierarchy permitted the disposal of those deemed *expendable* – the less fortunate swept under the moon's utopian facade.

Walker prepared the IV drip for another patient. After attaching a thin tube into the frail arm of a young boy, 100 cc of sparkling crimson flowed into his bloodstream. The stink of pungent antiseptic seeped through his mask's filter.

Mercer turned away from the patient as the serum coursed through the boy's body. She often boasted about how she had ice-cold water running through her veins, but deep down, it still got to her. She told herself that this was a *necessary* step for the progress of mankind. Much like the amputation of a rotting limb, an unpleasant procedure, but necessary for the good of the body. It did make it difficult to sleep seeing the young faces in pain, but that's when vodka came in handy.

Today had been a little *too exciting* for Mercer and would make for a hell of a lot of paperwork. Her colleague set down a fresh cup of coffee next to her desk.

Walker grumbled, "You know, it would be a lot easier if they weren't so young." Walker was complaining. What a surprise.

Mercer accepted the mug and ignored the invitation to dive into ethics. "Almost ready to start testing on adults." Maybe some will *actually* survive.

Walker took another sip from the steaming cup.

"This is a big fuckin' deal."

The progress of man had always been written in death. Every step forward, every safety protocol had been written in blood. It was rather easy to find people for this research. What was it that Kessler called them? Bottom feeders. There were millions of souls on Ganymede alone and resources were slim this far from the Sun. If someone caused problems, or were rather unwilling to pull their weight, they were easily disposed of. This was an unwritten rule enforced by all the local authorities. Not so much *enforced* as ignored. If the undesirable was disposed of, the local governments rarely, if ever, enforced any punitive action against the defendant. Of course, there were ways to explain that a problematic person was no longer a nuisance. Polite company would say that they were serving a life sentence; consigned to manual labor at the Jovian Correctional Facility on Io. She presumed that only

3

children and the optimistically naive really believed that nonsense.

These shifts had been long but Walker was right, they were onto something big. One of the children stirred and their vital signs fluctuated on the monitors. The doctors turned to the table. White residue crusted around the child's lips. Their arms wretched taut against the strap holding him in place. Mercer's lips tightened into a thin line.

"This might be it," said Walker.

The child's bloodshot eyes flickered open.

2

MANKIND HAS DOMINATED THE SOLAR SYSTEM. SETTLEMENTS, nations, and the inevitable territory disputes have reached well past the Gas Giants to the Kuiper Belt. Presently, the United Jovian Systems holds a vice grip on commerce as the premier authority for governance and traffic for the icy moons of Jupiter.

The largest moon of Jupiter is Ganymede. It's made up of several nations and city-states, with the most prominent being the UJS and GR territories. On the Western side of the curtain stood the fledgling nation of the Ganymede Republic.

Kepler City sat comfortably beneath the looming shadows of the steep crater rims. The city dome was composed of ultra-strong triangular segments, each no wider than a meter. It was erected from diamond sheets fortified with layers of graphene that created an additional magnetic field to protect against Jupiter's radiation belt.

A constellation of satellites adjusted their trajectories in low orbit above Ganymede and released a ballistic projectile. The metallic behemoth hurtled down from the heavens. The telephone pole sized projectile made with pure tungsten steel. A kinetic bombardment device, colloquially known as "The Rod from God." The cylindrical projectile descended with a relentless velocity, aimed at the heart of Kepler City.

The Rod from God hit the city dome with a force of .3 megatons after free falling for 5 minutes. The force from this impact was 20.9 times more powerful than the 15 kiloton atomic bomb dropped on Hiroshima over half a millennia prior.

The orbital bombardment struck through the transparent dome surrounding Kepler City with a deafening boom. Cracks from the crumbling impact hole sprawled through the transparent sheets and took seconds before any discernible drop in atmospheric pressure was detected by the life support program.

An automated pressure switch activated immediately and deployed an instantly inflated gas capsule to wedge the breach. Something dropped from a man-made satellite was always a possibility that they had a contingency plan for as kinetic weapons had been used throughout various conflicts on Earth but never out here. The problem with *The Rod from God* was not merely that it punctured the city dome, but that it carried with it the destructive power of a meteor strike. An immediate system collapse within seconds.

The rod created a flash of light when it pierced through the dome barrier, caused by the intense friction and heat generated upon contact with the internal atmosphere. It was terribly loud. Nearby eardrums ruptured and the intense light emitted during the impact fried the retinas of anyone observing. Those poor souls suffered instant flash blindness. There was a sudden release of energy upon contact with the embassy building. The shockwave propagated outward from the impact and any person within the impact radius instantly vanished in bright violence. The wave caused intense over pressurization of the immediate area, and buildings and infrastructure within the blast radius crumbled.

The shockwave continued to reverberate throughout the periphery. Frantic citizens screamed. Structures crumbled. The city once referred to as *The Paris Past the Belt* lay in ruins.

3

"WHAT I DON'T GET IS *WHY* THEIR OWN EMBASSY?" ASKED THE news anchor to journalist Kate Abara in a separate shot. The morning broadcast was being played from the corner monitor in the office.

"We don't know who did this-"

"C'mon. It's pretty apparent."

"-but, could they have targeted the embassy due to resentment? Working with *the oppressor* kind of thing? Not saying we are the oppressor, but that's what *they've* convinced themselves of."

"If you want to make an omelet, you've got to crack a few eggs."

"Collateral damage? That's certainly a possibility, Amber."

"That's what I'm thinking."

The Jovian National News (JNN) and other sensationalized broadcast networks wasted no time pointing fingers at the

Ganymede Republic. Accusations ran wild of masterminding the attack on Kepler City. Wasn't it obvious? The allegations repeated throughout various talking heads across every broadcast network.

The Defense Intelligence Agency is the United Jovian System's foreign intelligence department headquartered in Roosevelt, Ganymede. Their sole responsibility is to consolidate, analyze, and communicate information between the military, the executive branch, and national security departments by collecting and analyzing foreign intelligence to support national security decisions.

A handful of stressed out staff members sat in a briefing room in the Defense Intelligence Agency. Above the main doorway was a plank with the phrase engraved into it with a daily reminder to the reason they were here. It read:

THIS IS NOT ABOUT YOU

As Deputy Director of Operations, Samuel J. Thornton was a seasoned professional. Across the table from Thornton sat Asher Cohen and Alex Turner, fellow analysts and field operatives with reputations for getting the job done. Turner always had on the latest fashion attire which Cohen always wondered how he afforded it on a modest field officers' salary, but assumed he was most likely in massive credit debt.

Thornton turned off the news monitor in the corner of the room and addressed his top operatives. "GRPA is the first suspect for the Kepler City attack. I want a comprehensive analysis of their recent activities, contacts, and possible motives. Turner, I need you to gather any actionable intelligence. We cannot afford to take action without being sure.

"Westies claim full transparency, denying any involvement in Kepler City and *supposedly*, they're just as surprised as we are. I'm not sure if I buy it. Cohen, I need you to find out if there's a chance this is an independent faction acting."

"Wilco, sir."

"Any news from your friend in SIS?"

Cohen cleared his throat and spoke up. "There's a lack of internal chatter indicating any involvement. Kepler City's defense satellite appears to have been compromised, but it's not clear how."

Turner added in, "It might be a coding issue, a freak accident. I'll dive deeper to rule out any foul play."

"What about the GRPA?"

During the revolution, the Ganymede Republic formed the Ganymede Republic Provisional Army (GRPA). The GRPA is a paramilitary organization dedicated to achieving the reunification of Ganymede by force. They are the de facto armed forces branch of the Ganymede Republic, even though they unofficially act without Congressional approval and oversight. This remained a point of attrition but Ganymede has bigger fish to fry at the present moment. Their initial goal was to end the United Jovian System rule and to establish a fully autonomous Ganymedean state through extreme violence.

Turner sighed as he pushed himself from the desk and bounced his pencil off the table in front of them. In the low gravity it slowly floated off in an arc towards the ground as he made a frustrated noise. In 1965 CE, Paul C Fisher spent over one million dollars and *10 years* of research and development to engineer a pen with a pressurized ink cartridge that would be able to write in microgravity and extreme conditions. The creative Russians reportedly solved this issue by simply using a pencil.

He shook his head and responded, "The GRPA *is* showing increased activity, but their communications remain guarded. It's challenging to discern their true intentions. They might be leveraging the situation to their advantage."

"Keep digging. We need answers before this escalates any further. This can't be another Tharsis incident."

Cohen's eyes never left the screen as he read out loud. "The Castrum," the formal name of the executive office building for the GR capitol in Derry, "is genuinely surprised. Internal communications show no signs of involvement. A defense satellite breach seems more like a technical glitch than a deliberate act. Still, I'm running diagnostics to be certain."

"Good. I need it by the books. The Director is on my ass." A report released through an anonymous source claimed that the 'attacks will continue until Olympus is free.' DIA had already checked the report, it was unsubstantiated and the source had not been verified.

"Turner, got anything?"

"Increased activity from the GRPA, but their motives remain unclear. I don't know, Sam. I think they're exploiting the situation to rile up their base."

Cohen reported, "I'm isolating anomalies, sir." He paused. "This *might* be a distraction." An alert blared from Cohen's terminal. "There's a discrepancy in the Orbital Defense Initiative protocols. It's subtle, but could be something deliberate."

Thornton asked, "Can you confirm that with our contacts in the SIS?"

Turner read aloud as he read the network broadcast, "GRPA denies involvement, acknowledges 'heightened readiness.' Whatever that means. Claims it's not their play, and they're willing to cooperate with all investigations."

"Fuck," Asher Cohen said. "Alright. This likely isn't GRPA. If it were, they wouldn't be so open to involvement and no way would they risk an attack on the UJS. We're talking war on god. Best bet is an independent actor."

"A terrorist faction?" Thornton asked.

"Has to be." Cohen responded. "I know things aren't perfect between UJS and the Ganymede Republic, but shit, it's a hell of a lot better than it has been."

"Could it be the Belt?"

"Unlikely. We haven't had any conflict with the Belt in years."

"Right. Well, not *direct* conflict."

"With the cease fire, there's no way this could be them."

"I don't *know* if it is them."

"I don't know, son. It's conspiratorial."

"No, it's not conspiratorial. It's a probability. A slim one, but a probability."

"I still don't buy it."

"All right, stay with me. Atomic weapons are banned per the treaty, right?"

"Right," agreed Cohen and Thornton.

"Kinetic weapons are fine. Therefore, dropping a rod is *technically* not violating the MAD treaty." Turner referred to the Mutually Assured Destruction Treaty that reduced weapons cache for both the Belt and UJS and banned the use of nuclear weapons.

"It *is* an act of war, which *is* illegal to do without Congressional approval for the Belt," said Cohen.

"Only if it's the state acting. If it's an independent faction acting, then it is terrorism, not state-sponsored action. I mean, it could be classified as *state-sponsored terrorism*."

"Okay. Let's assume it *is* an independent faction working. We need to find out who's behind it. Let's not let this escalate to a full-scale war."

Turner responded, "*If,* and it's a big if... *If* it's an independent faction, they might have different objectives. It *could* be the GRPA. I'm not ruling that possibility out. Whether they're Ganymede Republic, Belter, or maybe even someone not even on our radar, yet, we need to figure out their endgame."

Thornton spoke up, "Alright ladies. Don't jump to any conclusions. Here's the plan: First, Gather more intel." As he instructed each point, he struck an additional finger out. "Then find connexions. Uncover motives. Do not move until we have a clearer picture, is that understood?"

"Yes, sir," Asher and Turner confirmed in sync.

4

THE CHILD CONVULSED IN AN UNEXPECTED SURGE. THE VITAL signs cascaded into a rapid descent on the monitors. Mercer pulled open the child's eyelids, exposing bloodshot eyes to a beam of light from Mercer's flashlight. The child's pupils dilated and her tremors settled into stillness. Mercer and Walker continued to work through various fatality tests.

Walker checked his watch and pronounced, "Time of death is 0200."

When mankind first started conversing in lower orbit and the reaches of space, they had adopted Coordinated Universal Time (CUT). The time of day, whether you were in Greenwich, London, the research stations orbiting Venus, Mars, the Belt, or the Jovian System would all be Coordinated Universal Time.

Mercer removed her gloves. "Alright. Nothing more we can do. Put the body on ice and write up the report."

"Got it. I'll have it on your desk by lunch."

Walker diligently resumed his documentation and spoke into his note recorder after scrubbing his hands raw. "The A2 variant demonstrates a 61% mortality rate, 14% non-reactionary, and 25% positive reactivity." Progress, but not quite reaching the intended mark yet.

5

ELSIE HARPER FINISHED HER THIRD CUP OF COFFEE IN THE SMALL windowless office. The analyst would drip cold brew straight into her veins if she could. She worked hunched over, a trait that her mother made continuous efforts to correct her poor posture over the past forty years.

Multiple small desks cluttered the room before a large display screen that showcased maps, intelligence reports, and potential leads. Clark Andrews, her mustachioed partner in the department with a deformed cauliflower ear, and a handful of intelligence officers for the Ganymede Republic's Special Intelligence Service (SIS) sat at a cheap synthetic-wood table.

A seasoned field operative, Luis Hernandez asked, "What about Krasnyy? He was involved in the early days of *Pugna Nostra*. Could he be linked to this?"

The separatist movement known as Pugna Nostra, Our

Fight, had previously elected a super majority of representatives to govern the most Western districts of Ganymede when it was still a part of the United Jovian System. Instead of assimilating into the UJS Congress, they declared independence and established the Ganymede Republic. The UJS imposed martial law for the next few years in a futile attempt to quash the secessionist movement. The Belter Empire was the first to officially recognize the Ganymede Republic as an independent nation. The Belt never officially declared war against the UJS but rather focused on weakening its borders by supporting the Ganymede Republic through financial aid, trade, and an influx of weaponry to the rebels. The UJS reluctantly recognized the Western districts' independence years ago in an attempt to resolve the escalating tensions with the Belt.

"No. Anton Krasnyy has been off the radar for two years."

Andrews assured, "I'll keep an eye out to see if anyone knows anything on Krasnyy and keep you updated."

"Any more news on HAMMERHEAD?" Hernandez tried to steer the discussion back to brainstorming. He had what was considered a wiry frame. Tall with a strong jawline, he was clean shaven with a tightly trimmed haircut that he had been sporting since his active duty days.

"I've almost got enough to take back to Devis. There's the usual noise online, but nothing verified. The most extreme are convinced that Kepler City was sabotaged by their own. And there is this new group flagging up called *Ganymede First*."

"I've heard of that," Ramirez said.

"Yeah, I'm not sure if it is connected to the RFG but I'm not ruling it out. Do we know how it dropped, yet? Where was it remotely activated from?"

"Yeah, I've been searching for that." Ramirez again. "It was dropped from a satellite in their Orbital Defense Initiative program. Someone bypassed the security network and safe-guards. I think the only way this could work-"

"Someone on the inside working with them?"

"Yeah, like I said, it's not concrete, but this is what I'm thinking. Someone internally was able to override the defense satellite, trigger the weapon, and override all the fail safe protections preventing an accidental code-error or weapons malfunction. This operation must've taken a long time to set up."

Andrews speculated, "If someone was trying to make a political message, or specific point, or fuck, even in protest for some bullshit cause they were willing to die for, they would likely already have made a definitive statement."

"Maybe Black Knife," suggested Harper, referring to an extreme paramilitary terrorist group. "They've been pretty quiet since they blew up that courthouse in New Kandahar."

Hernandez corrected, "No. The courthouse was a one-man operation."

Andrews replied, "It's not Black Knife. We have an asset higher up with them. Devis would have been informed."

"Maybe not if it would compromise them as a source," said Ramirez. You really only get one big action before your cover is blown as a spy.

Andrews firmly replied, "No. With something this big,

they're trained to let us know and we arrange an immediate extraction. Once something like this is leaked, that asset is no longer safe or guaranteed as reliable. It is better for them to be discerning in the information they pass along. Besides, this really isn't their style. They always upload a public statement after an attack."

"Who are you thinking?" asked Harper.

Ramirez spoke as she read directly from a social network on her terminal, "There is a Ganymede First rally happening this weekend outside the convention center here in town. Ali Miller is speaking." Ali Miller was a lionized internet activist known for extreme rhetoric who had been banned from a majority of social networks for inflammatory comments.

Andrews asked, "Ali Miller? The dude who said chemicals in the water supply-"

"-turn people into subservient consumers? Yeah. That lunatic," finished Harper.

"Or that prison on Io is just a front for a death camp."

"You know, he's actually right on occasion," Ramirez interjected.

"Here we go," Andrews said.

"Don't be so closed minded. He was telling people about the Belter's involvement with the Rockwell arms deal months before that came to light."

Andrews scorn Ramirez, "Ali Miller is divorced from reality. You work in intelligence, Maria. He's dangerous. Don't be so open minded that your brain falls out."

"I'm not saying he's a *reliable* authority for information."

"He *is* an imbecile," continued Harper. She prided herself as very open-minded, but right now she felt like a bitter old man.

"Well. He's a *useful idiot* to us. Find out what you can. Let's run this by Devis, and find out what we can," directed Hernandez.

"Wilco."

This was hopefully a step in the right direction.

6

THE DISTANT MORNING GLOW FROM JUPITER FILTERED THROUGH the glass windows. Alex Turner and Asher Cohen sat and hunched over their desks with eyes glued to glowing monitors in the DIA headquarter building in Roosevelt.

"What I don't get is how they broke through these firewalls. Ganymede Republic doesn't have that tech."

"Can't you get the logs? I want to trace every single entry point. I'm not seeing any chatter on the darknet. A lot of people are screaming both for and against the attack, sympathizing for 'em, calling for us to nuke Derry. I can't believe these idiots are allowed to vote."

"I'm tracking it. Multiple points of entry using a VPN, encrypted signatures." Virtual proxy networks are often used to hide your IP address online by scrambling your unique computer signature.

"VPN? That's untraceable normally, isn't it?"

"Not quite. We have a few options here that we'd have to run by Thornton and Freeman, but the department could compel the VPN provider to disclose user information. They should keep logs and are subject to our jurisdiction. We should try that first, but they're likely to not be that dumb. Most likely double encrypted. I'll deep dive to detect patterns or behaviors associated."

"What about finger painting?"

"Fingerprinting? That's what I'm referring to. Identifying users based on their unique configurations and patterns. Fortunately for us, they accessed the satellite off-planet. The program is showing remote access from outside the grid."

Asher stared. "No one gets into a defense satellite like this without some serious hardware."

"Well someone did."

"That's the thing. They have gotten their hands on something beyond even *our* pay grade. Either there is a breakthrough in R&D that we don't know about, which is possible but slim, or they're getting outside help."

The boys fell silent. Had the game just shifted? The enemy may have played a card that no one predicted.

"Belter tech."

7

"POLICE SEARCH WARRANT! OPEN THE DOOR!"

A deafening blast crashed through the corridor as the top hinge surrendered to the powerful force. His arm tucked tight into his shoulder, the armored man aimed downward sharply at the middle hinges and released another round. The Rockwell 099 shotgun clicked as the forearm was pulled back, cocking the barrel and releasing the shells from the chamber at the middle hinge. Getting blasted point blank with a shotgun slug would neutralize any target. The shells hadn't even hit the floor before the second blast destroyed the second hinge on the apartment door. Two more blasts at the bottom hinge freed the door from any constraints as shards of synthetic wood drifted down in the low gravity. The officer leaned back and threw his weight forward into the heel of his foot as it slammed into the unsupported door. The door flew back into the immediate wall behind, then bounced to the ground. This took less than 4 seconds total from the first trigger pull to when the fractured door hit the ground.

On queue, another operator released the trigger on a flash grenade into the apartment. All the operators outside the apartment briefly turned their eyes away for a split moment to protect against the flash. Magnesium powder filled the air inside the floor plan. The flash-bang produced a blinding light and a loud concussive noise. The intense light momentarily overwhelmed any vision, while the loud bang created a disorienting effect. This combination was intended to confuse and temporarily incapacitate potential threats, allowing the team to swiftly secure the area with reduced resistance.

"Move!" commanded the operator for the Special Weapons and Tactics (SWAT) team in Lansing, UJS Ganymede. The team rushed in.

"Fire!"

"Fire!" screamed another.

The flash bang had set a small fire in the corner of the room. The lights were off in the apartment. One of the operators checked the doors and corners, then ran to the corner to stomp it out. The only lights in the small apartment were the flames of the furniture, a small flickering television program on the wall, and the flash lights on their weapons.

A young child was in the living room laying down on the ground while the television was blasting cartoons of talking animals. The child was frantic and confused by the commotion.

"Up, up, up!" yelled an officer with a shotgun aimed at the child's face.

The child dashed up.

"Hands on top of your head! Hands on top of your head!"

The child obeyed as operators ran past her. An officer remained with his weapon drawn at the kid, with another performing a Terry frisk.

The SWAT officers were head to toe in tactical gear. They fanned out through the apartment. Their movements were calculated and synchronized as they crept through each hallway. After checking a room, each operator investigating would yell that it was clear. DIA operatives Turner and Cohen stormed in wearing bulletproof vests over crisp Oxford shirts.

Covert actions are typically executed by the same officer/s who gathered the intel. They spend about three-quarters of their time collecting information and the remainder in covert operations.

Both intelligence officers had their standard issue Laika RD-2 pistols drawn in the two handed Weaver stance, with the dominant arm straight and the other arm bent, both hands firmly on the pistol to support and guide each tentative shot. As the team cleared the rooms, it became evident that the house was empty (with the exception of the unsupervised child). After the apartment had been declared vacant of threats, the officers holstered their weapons as the policemen questioned the little one.

Turner cussed.

"Turns out the kid is just some neighbor's kid who came

over to watch cartoons. Otherwise, this place has been vacant for weeks. Overall, bad intel."

Turner shook his head, "Maybe not bad." His face shrunk. "Outdated."

"Someone tipped them off," Cohen proposed.

This was their second raid that had yielded the same result—empty rooms. The SWAT team regrouped outside.

"This is the second time we've gotten bad intel. That's actually pretty on par with average. Informants aren't always reliable. Maybe they have got someone on the inside."

"It's possible the department is compromised. We should grab a comprehensive list of everyone who might have access to the office, including myself, and do a thorough audit line by line. No exceptions. Even our cleaning staff requires security clearance and anyone could be compromised."

The room was a cold, sterile space of stainless steel and bright lighting. Dr. Viktor Kessler watched the data on the holographic display. He typed commands into the console. Dr. Michael Walker stood beside him as Dr. Jesssica Mercer worked in the office.

The culmination of their research stood before them—a room housing subjects transformed into rabid figures, twisted manifestations of their morbid ambition.

The subjects now thrived in a state of pure instinct, a condition designed to enhance their aggression to unprecedented levels. Walker remained apathetic as one of the subjects tore into the remains of an animal, a macabre display of their success. He listened as Kessler detailed the potential applications of the weapon.

Subject A was frenzied and primal. It lunged at the remnants of flesh and blood. Kessler and Walker watched the visceral Subject A tearing meat off the bones. Blood splattered across the pristine floor. As the red droplets painted what was left, Walker noticed the remnants of a shirt labeled SUBJECT F.

A few days later, a SWAT team approached the target building under the cover of darkness. Intel broke this down as the last location for the VPN addresses that Turner discovered, and frustration begrudged their every step. It splintered open with the third strike against the door with a battering ram. The team stormed in with weapons drawn, gun stocks firmly tucked into their shoulders with the barrel just below chin height.

Rooms, shadows, and likely danger waiting in the apartment. They had gotten lucky in the previous raids as no one was hurt. That would change. The team began to clear each room.

A door on the other end of a hallway slammed shut. This demanded the SWAT teams' attention. The terrorists had been waiting.

An officer yelled, "Police! This is the police! Make yourselves visible and keep your hands where we can see them!"

Another officer shouted, "If you're inside make yourself known. Walk towards the sound of my voice!"

The officers cautiously stepped towards the door. The second officer put his hand on the back of the body armor of the leading commander to signal he was behind him. He reminded him in a calm tone, "Slow."

A bedroom door in the hallway breached. The two terrorists stood in the doorway, adorned with explosive vests. The SWAT team pointed rifles tucked in their shoulders, directly aimed at their faces.

"Freeze! Get on the ground!" commanded an officer.

Simultaneously, the officer behind him yelled, "I will shoot you in the head. You're going to - you're going to die right now! I will shoot you!"

One terrorist ignored the order and turned to run back into the room. He didn't make it to the door.

Elsie Harper focused on the screen displaying lines of code and data. The Deputy Director of Operations worked at another table behind her.

"Got something," Elsie announced.

Devis leaned closer to scrutinize the data. It shifted. Harper traced a few consistent connections mapping back to Vanguard Solutions. She explained how she traced the signal to Callisto and messages sent to the Vanguard Solutions research department.

"You're smarter than you look, Elsie."

"Thanks! Wait. What?"

Devis smirked and said, "Send Clark in. Have him sniff around."

"Stay back!" the lead terrorist barked, fingers twitching above the detonator. The SWAT team poured in behind them, a wave of body armor, high-octane testosterone, and fierce men. Their weapons aimed at the bomber. The officers were all shouting.

"Get on the ground!"

"Drop it! Drop to the ground!"

"Get down!"

His friends' body lay next to him on the ground. It was so loud he couldn't think. The terrorist realized the diminishing window of opportunity and made a split-second decision. He yelled, "Sic semper tyrannis!" The terrorist clenched his teeth and pressed the detonator in his right hand.

The SWAT commander moved to close in on the terrorist. The suspect was disoriented and surrounded. He offered no resistance as the commander and his team closed the distance. The commander's gloved hands moved to secure the suspect's wrists with plastic restraints.

In a gruff voice, the officer grunted, "Game over, creep." In adherence to protocol, the bomber then had his rights recited to him. The homemade suicide vest had been a dud to the relief of everyone, including the man currently being held down.

8

IT IS A COMMON MISCONCEPTION THAT ALL EMPLOYEES WITHIN A specific intelligence department are titled agents. An *agent* is a foreign asset who is recruited to work against their own country in concert with another country's intelligence department. An *officer* is a citizen who works faithfully for their own country's intelligence agency, whether domestic or abroad. An example of an agent would be if someone who worked for the Belt gave privileged information about the Belt to the DIA in exchange for money and certain privileges, such as access to superior healthcare procedures. An example of an officer would be if a citizen of the UJS were to work for the DIA and provided privileged information about the Belt to the DIA, whether by intercepting information or through information being obtained via agents.

While the DIA itself does not have police enforcement

privilege, they are able to operate domestically if the operation concerns foreign special information.

Papers and maps cover a cluttered desk in a dimly lit apartment. The phone on the desk began to ring. The light from the specific phone terminal indicated it was a secure landline. Cellular conversations were child's play to intercept. The agent set down a map before answering.

"Yeah?"

"Is everything still in motion?"

The agent checked a map of New London pinned on the wall behind the desk.

"Yeah. It's all set as planned."

"Good. *The Boss* wants to meet on Thursday at the usual time."

"Understood."

"Don't be late."

"I never am."

The line went dead. The agent set the terminal down and walked to the window in their office. The enormity of Jupiter's colorful swirls devouring the horizon. The city lights glimmered like distant stars. The agent turned back to the desk and shuffled through the papers until a picture of Timothy Jones was placed on top.

9

"Sergeant Cohen? Uh... Asher is in here."

Elsie Harper was guided into the DIA office, scanning the room for him. She spotted the man near a cluster of desks and approached him without a word.

"You son of a bitch." She dropped the file onto his desk. Asher stood up, wrapped his long limbs around and gave Elsie the biggest bear hug, picking her off the ground.

"You two know each other?" asked Asher Cohen's coworker Kelly.

Harper recited, "We served together on the best god damned unit that the UJS had ever seen!"

"Yes ma'am. B Company, 1st Battalion of the 506th High Altitude Low Orbit Jumpers of the 103rd Airborne Division. Two tours together out in the big empty. B Company was a damn fine company."

"Damn fine!"

"Ah, I had no idea. Kindred spirits, then?"

"Best friends!"

"When you serve with someone, you get to know them real well, is all. Harper is practically my sister at this point."

"A sister who you still owe money to."

"That was like eight years ago."

Harper shrugged.

"You're never going to let that bet down are you?"

"Not until you pay up, Sarge."

There was a pause of awkward silence.

"Well. Hooah, you two." Kelly laughed quietly and went back to her desk.

"It's Ooorah," Harper corrected as Kelly was walking off, he waved a hand in the air in acknowledgement.

They each grabbed a coffee and sat around his desk. After briefly covering small talk, they got to the meat of the matter.

"We're not investigating the GRPA on the attack on KC. Well, we did and didn't find any leads. If it is someone in the Western districts, we know that they are acting without state endorsement. At least, without *public* state endorsement."

"It doesn't make sense for it to be the Ganymede Republic."

"I know. As happy as I am to see an old friend, why are you here?"

Harper pointed at the dossier in the folder she had plopped on his desk. "What do you know about Anton Krasnyy?"

"Political figure for the Belt. Former propagandist. Worked in the communications department. Questionable ethics and practices. I haven't heard any news about him. At least, nothing that I'm cleared for, anyways."

"Krasnyy is a master of propaganda. He's very good at influencing people's thoughts and beliefs. He was the one who started the *Only Belters Bleed* campaign a few years back that garnered disdain against UJS. The Belt sent him to Derry to be useful." Cohen leaned forward with attention as she spoke. "The Belt didn't *officially* say they were helping the Western districts. Ceres sent Krasnyy to assist in the fight for independence. Except he was *too extreme*, even for the radicals in the GRPA. Any revolutionary could be considered a war criminal by the parent company, but there's a fine line between freedom fighting and well... let's just say he was too much for the GRPA. He was kicked out."

"Have you heard anything from him? There haven't been any confirmed declarations."

"No, we haven't heard anything from him for years. But, I think he was involved in KC and based on word on the street, there's another operation in planning."

"You know we found that the RFG was hacked using Belter tech?"

"Why would the Belt fund an attack directly on UJS? That would be suicide."

"I know. I don't *know* if it's the Belt. But it's Belter tech. It's just so bizarre they're being quiet on this."

"The terrorists?"

Cohen typed on his terminal and a three-dimensional

holographic map of Ganymede projected above the conference table.

"Yeah. They have to be from the Western districts." He directed with his hand as he explained. "The two major UJS ports sitting directly East of Olympus are Kepler City here and New London." He drew an X on each city with his finger, which digitized on the hologram into red slash marks following the trace of his fingertips. "If I were to make a point, my next target would be New London."

10

I AM OFFICIALLY OLDER TODAY THAN MY FATHER WAS WHEN HE died, Clark Andrews thought to himself. The soft snow brushed against his visor on his helmet in the EVA suit. Equipped with a Laika 9 mm semi-automatic single-action pistol, and a Brahe 7.7 mm a bolt-action rifle with a modular designed high-powered armor-piercing fluted barrel, and a 1-6×24 mm scope for precise accuracy. He outfitted both weapons with silencers. With the atmosphere so thin on the surface of the Galilean moons, the benefit of the weapon is not silence outside a pressurized environment. Besides reducing the noise signature, suppressors also minimized recoil, improved accuracy by reducing muzzle rise, but most importantly, it eliminated muzzle flash. This is paramount in the dark wilderness of Callisto's surface where a bright light would draw unwanted attention. In the varied landscapes of his mission, Clark Andrews had equipped himself with an array of firearms designed for different ranges. For distant targets, he relied on long-barrel rifles, although Andrews didn't have one on hand during this mission. In the mid-range, ideal for distances up to 800 meters, fluted rifles were his weapon of choice. Fluting involves removing material from the barrel in the form of grooves or flutes. This reduces the overall weight of the barrel, making the firearm lighter and potentially more maneuverable while preventing overheating during rapid or sustained fire. As for close encounters within 25-50 meters, Andrews trusted his 9 mm pistol, a compact yet potent tool with lethal ballistics and an EMT discharge setting.

When Andrews was previously a Tier 1 Operator (Spec Ops), a sniper would be accompanied by five operators. Four of the operators would guard the rear from oncoming resistance, with the lead sniper on the target, and another next to them to help with precision measurements. When neutralizing a target from 1200 meters or more away, you need the assurance that a solid crew has your back. However, this was not a military operation. Although paramilitary in nature, and employed by a majority of former armed forces members, the SIS was strictly a civilian organization. This was a simple reconnaissance mission for counter-terrorism. This operation never *officially* happened.

460 kilometers West of the port he arrived in, between the nations of North Callisto and Verdeguay, Clark Andrews truly was in the middle of nowhere. He stood in the shadows

outside of enemy lines from the research facility. Something big was happening, it was drawing the attention of both the DIA and SIS. Andrews stood behind a rock in a crevice in a snowy mountain range. Callisto was the most distant Galilean moon of Jupiter. With a gravity of 1.2 m/s^2, which is 8% of 1G, Andrews was being held down, but not by much in the razor thin atmosphere. His EVA suit protected him from the radiation. The ever-imposing waning Jupiter hung in the horizon. In the valley of the mountain range lay satellite outposts just outside the research facility he had business at.

Andrews walked forward to the base of a satellite installation. The tower soared into the air from the barren mountain side juxtaposed with ancient, unmoving rock and man-made steel. At the top of the tower were six satellite dishes the size of three meters each, facing in three separate directions. The wind was starting to pick up. The atmosphere was too thin to carry sound, but he could still hear the sound of the wind gently blowing snowflakes against his tactical helmet. There was an industrial pipe jutting across a steep slope at the base of the rock, beneath the structure to the North to the other side of the narrow crevice. A dim light glowed where the pipe touched the wall. With how far he was from another person, a quick shot from his rifle destroyed the light and he quickly climbed up unseen onto the pipe.

In the far distance, another communication tower shone a bright flashing red light. Grasping the pipe to climb, Andrews straddled the cylindrical steel and positioned himself upright. Crouching to stay at minimum visibility, he ran across the top of the pipe being hidden by rising steam from a nearby vent. Climbing over a small ledge, he walked onto the snow covered rock on the other side of the crevice. Standing in a slightly crouched position as he walked against the dark rock kept his figure blending in with his environment. The dark pattern of his EVA suit had its advantages.

Walking slowly around a small bend, Andrews climbed down the ledge onto a lower plane, staying as small and as close to the dark rock walls as possible. As he crept forward, he came across an abandoned starfighter jet plane crashed on the ground. The starfighter was covered in snow with shattered glass from where the pilot self-ejected. It had been here for years. With no sound being carried in the environment, Andrews saw a spark of light against the fighter jet and a puff of white snow pushed into the air.

Do. Not. Get. Distracted. He chastised himself.

Andrews turned around to find someone with their hands raised in surprise to see him. Andrews pulled his rifle into his shoulder and the dual-point strap taut. He instantaneously lined up the threat into his iron crosshairs and pulled the trigger. The gun jammed. A spent casing had previously partially ejected and had become stuck in the ejection port.

Andrews scolded his machinery, "God damned piece of shit."

During the cursing, the threat stepped backwards, trying to diffuse the situation before he realized what was going on. They were not on the same radio comm-link, so there was no verbal communication available unless they physically touched helmets. No chance of that. After a moment of hesitation, the terrified operator scrambled to pull out a pistol from his holster. He shot at Andrews twice, missing both times. It was not clear if the patrolman was too nervous to shoot well, a terrible shot, or intentionally aiming poorly. One of the fundamental lessons you learn in the armed forces is that in combat, for the most part, humans do not want to kill other humans. A significant number of soldiers intentionally aim their weapons above the enemy's heads, choosing not to inflict harm due to the emotional difficulty of taking another human life. According to proven statistics, only around 15% of operators actively attempt to shoot at the enemy. Andrews was safely in that 15%.

Andrews pulled up his 9 mm pistol and pulled the trigger twice in rapid succession. The recoil was dampened due to the silencer. Two bullets hit the threat in the head. The guard collapsed as pink mist floated where they were just standing. Slowly falling down in the weak gravity. In the early morning, the dead operator's rifle hit the ground as the flashlight shone forward, alerting his crew. Two more people in tactical EVA suits scattered across the mountain side, visible by their bobbing flashlights as they ran. They were a mere 15 meters from Andrews.

He must have stumbled upon one of their patrol routes. God damned bad luck is all. He needed to get off their path. The two threats ran off around another corner, leaving Andrews back to the shadows as the wind picked up, howling against his helmet. He juked to the North and disappeared in the rocks and rubble of the mountain range. Once out of sight, he began to unjam his rifle. Just another Thursday back from his active duty days. Tap, Rack, Bang, he recited to himself. He firmly set the magazine by giving it a good whack. He racked the slide to eject the stovepipe and chambered a new round. He fired the weapon into the ground twice. Good as new. Time to move.

Andrews turned around another small bend and saw just a red lens flashlight attached to a rifle pointing straight down on the ground as someone was investigating. This was supposed to be a simple observation mission, just find out what is being planned and get out. Why was the installation so heavily guarded? If he knew there was this kind of manpower, he wouldn't have come alone. Hell, he wouldn't have even come at all. He worked field operations in espionage because he retired from active duty.

With a four second radio delay each way back to Ganymede, and a long round trip boat ride, he had to make the most of this opportunity. Time was not something to be wasted, and good men dying was a simple part of national defense. This was not war, but this was counter-terrorism. And terrorists are inherently at war with peace. Andrews justified to himself that if you have the ability to stop suffering of others, and choose not to, then you are an accomplice of that suffering yourself.

There was no other visible way to the research facility but through this narrow path. At least, no other way that kept

Andrews as anonymous as possible and kept this from becoming another *international incident*.

Andrews kneeled down, out of sight, and held up his rifle. Within the scope, it automated a distance of 110 meters to the target's head. In the crosshairs of the scope, a small digitized dotted line formed that automatically measured wind and atmospheric resistance for the optimal target path. Aiming slightly above the target's head and to the left, the digital line in the HUD dropped to their head. Andrews exhaled and pulled the trigger tight. At that very second, the kneeling operator bent over and the bullet missed. Shit. They stood up alert and fired a round in Andrews' direction. Obscured by darkness, he now had a clear shot at the patrolman. Aiming the crosshairs right between the eyes, he pulled the trigger twice. The body dropped to the ground. He was going to have to make this fast.

Just that second, another patrolman ran around the bend after seeing a fellow battle buddy hit the ground. It was very easy to see them coming with their bright flashlights attached to their rifles guiding the way. To Andrews' chagrin, above the body of the patrolmen he had killed, stood a watch tower blending into the mountain. None of these patrol installations are on the surveillance maps he had been studying. They blended in perfectly with the mountainous terrain from above. Surveillance satellites had not identified them.

Andrews set the crosshairs dead center on the silhouette figure as he stood behind a waist high stack of what appeared to be sandbags. Or, at least, regolith bags. He exhaled and pulled the trigger twice in succession as the twin bullets hit the man dead center in the face. One just inside his left cheek bone and the second right above the eyebrow ridge as he tumbled to the ground. The heat from inside the protective EVA suit steamed out of the cracks in the helmet to the frigid air of the moon. Andrews pulled the bolt on his rifle back as another bullet slid into position. Each magazine held 10 bullets.

A bright spark hit the rock in front of his face. He quickly turned to his right to see the flash of a muzzle in the distance. Andrews was knocked onto the ground by a blunt force that took the breath out of him. He immediately crawled on the ground behind a boulder for cover. The early morning lit up as bullets sparked on the rocks surrounding him. He hid until the sentry's magazine emptied. As soon as there was a respite in the volley, Andrews leaned to the right of the rock he was positioned behind and delivered two bullets into the torso of the enemy, who promptly slumped forward.

Andrews paused to double check and confirm the coordinates on the map on his terminal. He quickly searched the still warm corpse, took any credits and his facility ID. Andrews slid them into a small pouch on his utility belt and pulled out a repair patch. The projectile that hit him did not pierce the bullet proof vest built into his EVA suit. A tiny hiss of air steamed out from the puncture hole the ballistic created. Pressing the adhesive patch over the hole created a temporary seal and secured the pressurization and internal environment of the suit. After searching himself over for any more holes, he pressed on around a ridge.

A guard tower lingered above. At the feet of the tower were two guardsmen facing opposite his direction shining a flashlight into a crevice. One of the companions guided another flashlight around the darkness. Andrews knelt lower and decided to remain unseen. As the men were distracted searching, he lurked in the darkness along the perimeter of their watch. Andrews cursed. Directly in front of him, just walking past within a meter's distance, was a heavily guarded trooper with a 5.6 mm Squad Automatic Weapon (SAW). This close and without heavy armor, Andrews would be dead meat. For fortune's chance that the guardsmen just missed seeing him and kept walking onward, perpendicular direction of Andrews. He took advantage of the luck and picked up his pace towards the base.

After fast-paced trodding, the path narrowed to a flat wall between crevices. Andrews tossed a rope to the top of the flat 3 meters above him. The automatic anchor in the rope bolted into the rock to secure a brief rappel. He quickly scurried up. If this were a recreational hike, he would simply use his thrust pack to bounce up; the light created from a thrust pack would be quite apparent in the darkness. With Callisto's low gravity, someone could theoretically jump high enough without the need of a thrust pack, but a thrust pack would help direct your trajectory through the air. Someone could also easily overshoot the jump and be exposed. As he dropped down over to the other side, he saw a frozen river of liquid methane. He double checked the map and coordinates. The information he needed to download was just in the facility across the river bed. A subsequent and repeating click triggered in his ear, which alerted him that he was beginning to be picked up on a turret scanner. Andrews dropped to his knees and scoured the distance to find where the sensor was. He kept his body as low to the ice as possible as he scurried across to the other side of the frozen river.

Climbing up onto the rock side, there was a brief climb to see the facility. The river ice and the path opposite were lit by the bright aurora lights in the sky. Turning down the path, there he saw the facility. Whatever this information was, it was too sensitive to be trusted on a shared network. It had to be contained through hard drives. The building ahead had four short towers of buildings, roughly 2 to 3 stories tall. A guardsman paced side to side on the second story. Another guardsmen was posted in front of the gate entrance. The facility was surrounded with a chain-linked fence and dim lighting. The snow began to pick up as the winds howled against Andrews' helmet. Now or never. Sprinting down to the base of the path he had taken on the back-end of the facility, he turned around to see two men standing at the base of the main road. A quick draw of his rifle and two seconds later, two figures dropped to the ground as pink mist slowly floated down in the low gravity. Walking towards the side-entrance gate, there was a broken snow-mobile billowing dark smoke into the sky. He paused at the gate and pulled out his 9 mm pistol. He paced forward in the weaver stance. Andrews clicked a switch on the anterior side to activate the pulse electromagnetic transient (EMT) battery. As he sat just out of sight, Andrews aimed at the camera just above the gate and pulled the trigger. A 100 milliwatt pulse fried the closed circuit television (CCTV) camera. 50 milliwatts was enough to temporarily blind a camera. 100 milliwatts would fry the circuitry to disable it. This is one of the many fundamental distinctions as to why you should never send a machine to do a man's job. With Belter-made tech, a robot can be hacked mid-mission or stopped simply by a concentrated EMT wave. To be fair, a human can be simply stopped by a bullet. There are pros and cons to both. Weaponized machines, such as armed drones or gun-bearing robots, along with the use of atomics have all been outlawed by international law. It would be naive to think that simply because something is illegal it won't be pursued. Being caught manufacturing or using a weaponized machina is an easy way to find yourself doing manual labor at a correctional facility on Io.

A guardsman had been working on the machine, set down his tool, and ran inside his office to grab something. The facility was not on lockdown and they had not discovered his presence yet, but that was only a matter of time with the bodies piling up and the CCTVs going offline. Andrews took advantage of the brief errand and bolted past the side-entrance gate, ducking behind the snow-mobile until the coast was clear. He shot a pulse at the next security camera and sprinted into one of the tower entrances. He held the ID card against the external terminal as it flickered from red to green to allow access. He hit the trigger to enter the airlock, which opened after what seemed to be a lifetime. Inside the airlock for the facility, Andrews closed the outside door as the small room pressurized. As the room filled with oxygen and livable pressure, sound began to return. Once the room was cleared, a bright green light turned on above the door and Andrews heard a buzzer signaling it was safe to enter.

NASA once referred to a spacesuit as a 'space-craft for one person.' An EVA suit is a contained environment. Humans evolved to live in a very thin layer of Earth's atmosphere and this was a way to provide protection from the environment and internal homeostasis away from our home world and from the safety of pressurized habitats. Clark Andrews always kept his helmet on in the field. There are plenty of reasons to keep your helmet on in space. First and foremost, atmospheric gas can creep into any habitat without proper air scrubbers. A prolonged lifetime exposure to these gasses carries the minimum risk of being carcinogenic and the maximum peril of convulsions, loss of consciousness, and imminent death. Most of his colleagues did not share this careful hesitation, but Andrews had learned first hand what can happen to someone when their 'safe' life support system is jeopardized.

In the most practical sense, a series of stray bullets could easily puncture the walls and jeopardize internal pressurization before equilibrium is achieved again. Andrews was better safe than sorry. He kept his EVA suit on and entered the facility immediately.

The floor within the building's bottom floor was a steel

grid. Andrews pulled up a slab and slid into the grid floor, closing the slab above him. As he carefully crept down the hall, he could see armed men walking and chatting above his head. Dirt from one of the guard's shoes scraped against the grid and crumbled onto Andrews' helmet face shield, partially obscuring his vision. He wiped it off, but it left a faint smear.

Andrews checked his terminal and the center tower he needed to access was only a few meters ahead. He waited until there were no guardsmen around, and opened the grid panel above his head. He was directly under an oscillating CCTV camera. Just out of view, he quickly climbed out of the floor and left the panel in its original place. Andrews clicked the pistol back into ballistics mode, the mechanics of the weapon made a small electronic whimper as it shifted back into place. Running around the corner hall, he found stairs on the other side. As he began to climb the stairs, a figure walking down the stairs made eye contact. Startled, the enemy scrambled to pull out their pistol but were stopped by two 9 mm bullets into their gut by accident. The shot was intentional while the placement was not. Depending on what organs were hit, a gut wound can often take anywhere between one hour and seven days before the wounded eventually die. As the man that Andrews shot slid to the ground, the wall smeared deep red behind him. His chest was taking quick and shallow breaths as bloodshot eyes peered at Clark Andrews. Andrews ended the suffering with a final shot to the forehead before moving on. One last open corridor between the stairs and the office he needed to enter. In front of the stairwell door was another oscillating camera that he took care of, and returned the weapon to ballistic mode. As he opened the door, another man was surprised on the other side. Andrews pulled the trigger and splattered the wall. He kept moving. He had already over-stayed his welcome and time was running out. In the next room, he opened the breaker box and flipped the lights off. His EVA suit helmet automatically shifted into night vision. Within the same office building, among the rows of tall computer towers, he found the computer terminal he needed. Andrews' helmet was configured for night vision compatibility, permitting him to read the information on the screen. A slightly transparent holographic rectangular display projected above the mechanical keyboard after he activated the machine. He inserted a data stick to the appropriate port and began to search for the information needed.

Andrews downloaded and encrypted the information to immediately broadcast it via the shared network to SIS on Ganymede through a satellite terminal. Once downloaded, the signal traversed a distance of 3000 kilometers to a geosynchro-nous communications satellite orbiting above Callisto. From there, it relayed back towards Ganymede. It completed the 1,883,000 km journey to Ganymede in approximately 4 seconds, with an additional 12 seconds elapsed before a confirming message returned. The confirmation was in the form of a double static click. The encrypted circuit was absent of obstructive static.

The entire time elapsed from first shot fired to broad-casting the uploaded file was only a few minutes. This was just brief enough a time window where no one would likely notice an absence of chatter on the comm signals, however there was not much time before an alarm would signal and the research facility would be on high alert. What is rather concerning to him was that for a benign research facility, it was heavily guarded. This was not your run-of-the-mill corporate espionage. This was beyond a reasonable amount of defense. Whatever was being planned, they wanted to keep this air tight, but did not have the means to attain trained soldiers to protect it. Which means this is not through a state, but another faction with a personal interest. Anyone can be armed with a rifle to pose a threat: simply point the weapon and pull the trigger. A true soldier requires patience and training. The intensity of the protective measures had to be a third-party's involvement. The fact that Andrews was so easily able to maneuver through these guards gave credence to their amateur training and discipline.

Despite his reputation as a marksman, Clark Andrews was no longer a professional sharpshooter. While such skills were occasionally requisitioned in fieldcraft, they paled in comparison to the demands of political assassinations or combat. In those cases, it was less of a one-man army sneaking in the shadows. During *the Troubles*, he would be perched 1600-2500 meters away from his target on the ground on a pad. The atmospheric pressure on these low gravity moons and dwarf planets is so minuscule that it would not have the same influence as a breeze, but the meager pressure remained sufficient to redirect a .50 caliber bullet. For fieldcraft, a .50 caliber would be considered overkill. Depending on the angle, it splattered a human head like a watermelon. In the context of espionage, a 7.7 mm was more than adequate for Andrews' nefarious but effective methods.

Clark Andrews was not yet free from danger. He had to get out of the facility and off-planet. Almost on queue, bright flashes filled the room above the door-way. The alarms squealed with a deafening siren inside the facility.

11

THE RIFLE WAS OUT OF AMMO AND CAST ASIDE. THE TWO MEN grappled in close combat, pitting one another against their grit and might. The operative reached down to grab his 18 cm high carbon steel combat knife sheathed on his leg. Doing so would be the last risk of his life.

Clark Andrews took the delay to withdraw his 9 mm pistol from the holster across his own vest. As the enemy drew the knife back for an underhand stab, Andrews grabbed the attacker's vest and held him tight. Almost like a close-grip hug. Hand to hand combat is high level problem solving with dire physical consequences. It often required unexpected actions and thinking outside the box to outsmart the enemy.

The enemy operative was not expecting the hug or the pistol now tucked neatly underneath his larynx. Three quick trigger pulls ended any further disagreement between the two of them.

After dropping the body, Andrews quickly ran through his options of disarming the alarm system. He didn't know where the alarm system was operating from. Even if he did, he didn't know the passcode. He wished he had a special operations gadget that neutralized all electromagnetic activity in the area, but then quickly thought about how stupid an idea that was. It would fry all his equipment in the process, and he definitely needed his EVA suit's life support system to get off this god-forsaken rock. Perhaps he could turn off the power which would disable the alarm system, but even then, he didn't know where the power box was. This operation really had gotten out of control.

Andrews cursed to himself and decided just to get out of sight as quickly as possible. The SIS field operator quickly ran to the airlock and cycled it. As the decompression chamber slowly worked, kept murmuring to the machine, "Go. Go. Go. Go. Go. Hurry up."

Outside the door, he could see two enemy guards searching the premises for the intruder. They were heading his way in haste. Clark Andrews ran like a bat out of Hell and scurried into the shadows of the mountain side.

Elsie Harper had originally discovered the trending patterns that caused SIS to send Clark Andrews to North Callisto. Now that he got what he came for, his only focus was to get out alive.

. . .

Kate Abara continued filming, unaware that he was closing in. On the walls next to her were various spray-painted latin phrases. She took photos of a vibrant red one spelling out "Noster dies veniet!"

The train station platform was bustling with commuters as Abara hunched over her camera to capture the atmosphere of the city. A discreet figure crept from behind.

Ganymede First's fight was for legitimacy. The world needs to see the struggle, to understand the cause. War journalists like Kate Abara were a double-edged sword. The movement needed them, but if they painted the peaceful protesters as villains, the world wouldn't listen, Timothy Jones told himself. He hid his tall and wide frame within the busy crowd. Jones watched Abara's camera, capturing the unrest in the background. The Ganymede Republic couldn't afford a negative image. Jones remembered what Krasnyy had taught him: anyone who was not in total support of the movement was complicit in UJS' oppression. There was an undeniable charisma about Krasnyy that drew people in, making them feel connected and inspired. He had dedicated his life to the cause. The Ganymede Republic's brothers and sisters of the Northern district were having their rights stripped away.

Olympians who desired to be reunited with the Western districts faced systemic discrimination in areas such as employment, housing, and voting rights. The electoral boundaries in Olympus were manipulated to favor loyalists to UJS leadership, leading to an unrepresentative government that did not reflect the demographic makeup of the population. The local government introduced internment without trial that primarily targeted individuals who sympathized with the Western district's fight for independence. The use of internment, house raids, and arrests without proper evidence escalated to further resentment.

Jones positioned himself near the edge of the platform with his eyes fixed on Abara as she worked. If journalists like her kept framing them as violent, they would lose the support they need to fight against their oppressor. The Ganymede First movement's focus was first and foremost to protect Ganymedeans from tyrannical rule.

It was obvious to Jones that Kate Abara had sided with the oppressors. In the past six months, Abara had written a smear campaign to sully the good name of the movement. Abara reported alleged human rights abuse being committed by Ganymede First, such as punishment beatings, killing snitches, racketeering, and extortion.

Abara saw Jones behind her in her peripheral vision, but it was too late. Jones shoved the frail woman off the ledge down onto the rails. The platform erupted in chaos. Jones turned casually, blending in with the frantic crowd. The train engineer's horn blared as the journalist scrambled to her feet. Abara was discombobulated from the forceful shove, the screaming horn, and the bright lights speeding towards her. She turned to run.

Kate Abara didn't even make it off the tracks.

12

"CLARK IS A DICK, BUT HE LOVES HIS COUNTRY," EXPLAINED ELSIE Harper.

"Was," replied Asher Cohen.

"Still getting used to that."

In the dimly lit office of the embassy, the heavy scent of coffee lingered in the recycled air as Cohen and Harper found themselves seated across a polished imitation mahogany table. Bona fide wood was almost impossible to find this far from Earth. Growing wood poses challenges due to limited space and the need for resource-efficient systems.

Cohen asked, "What do you call people from here, anyways? Someone from Callisto. Callisto*nian*? Callister? Callisto*nite*? Callisto*ni*? Cal-"

"*Callistan*," Harper interrupted his ramble. "It's Callistan,"

"Well, what about..."

"*Callistans*." Harper said after a moment's pause, "Do you

think sometimes you mask uncomfortable situations with humor?"

The two were interrupted as the door swung open. Harper gestured that they'd circle back to that observation. A dapper man greeted them. His sleeves were rolled up and had a coffee stain on his button-up (still drying from this morning's commute). The secretary gestured for the officers to sit.

"Welcome to North Callisto. The ambassador will join you shortly," he announced before retreating. He left the officers alone with the gentle hum of the life support system.

There were many nations and city-states on most of the moons of Jupiter. Although considered a UJS territory, North Callisto was considered a protectorate. A protectorate maintains its status as an independent state, while its external affairs are overseen by the protecting country.

In spite of the frozen tundra of the moon, it was unusually hot in the hab, and everyone seemed to have sweat marks beneath their arms and neck. Except Harper. She was still cold. Harper was *always* cold. Her partner often complained that her toes felt like frozen slugs underneath the bed sheets.

With the time-sensitive situation, the DIA and SIS joined together in a temporary alliance to expedite the investigation.

"Shit," Cohen remarked, breaking the initial silence as he reached for the offered coffee. It was Navy coffee, robust and bitter, traditionally brewed on naval ships. Made with a high ratio of ground coffee to water and sometimes a pinch of salt is added to reduce acidity. It certainly wasn't as good as the coffee the intelligence drones driving desks were drinking.

"They certainly don't spare any expense on the caffeine here," he said with heavy sarcasm.

Harper shook her head.

"Be nice."

Although, she was similarly not impressed by what she was drinking, if you could even call the black sludge in her cup coffee.

As Harper was picking the grain of a ground coffee bean out of her teeth, the door creaked open once again. The ambassador entered this time. If you could hear a piano fall, you could hear her footsteps. A middle-aged woman with a warm smile extended a handshake to each of them in succession.

"Dr. Harper. Officer Cohen. Thank you for joining me today. I'm Charlize Petrov. I trust you've settled in?"

"Yes, thank you, Ambassador," Harper replied.

"Petrov. Any relation to Lev Petrov?" asked Cohen.

"The pilot?" asked Harper.

"Yeah, the one who flew the slingshot around Saturn."

"Jupiter," Petrov corrected.

Cohen continued, unbothered, "...Jupiter hitting like twenty-eight hundred km per hour."

"Twenty-six, two hundred," Petrov corrected again.

"I read about that!" Harper said with excitement. "They thought it was physically impossible in a single-person cruiser and he broke all those records. They had to rewrite astrophysics textbooks."

"Well, *they* certainly say a lot of things. Don't they?"

commented the ambassador.

"Did you hear about what happened after he got back?"

"Well, yeah. That's why I asked her concerning the aftermath of what happened with his parents and the-"

Petrov politely interjected to shut the conversation down further: "Unfortunately and well, fortunately, no. We are not related. No affiliation." She smiled at the duo.

Cohen did an about-face and dropped the topic. The three were seated around the desk. On the ambassador's desk were a keyboard, a holoprojected screen display, pictures of friends and family, and a little replica UJS flag. It was primarily red with blue and gold highlights.

"Before we begin, everything we are about to discuss is confidential. I want to stress the utmost importance of discretion in what we're about to reveal. It remains strictly between us. Do you mind telling me what the fuck your field officer was doing on my moon without permission? In case you weren't aware, crossing into another country illegally and committing numerous acts of violence, including killing multiple people, are all serious criminal offenses. We have the legal authority to prosecute and adjudicate these crimes."

"We have reason to believe that a significant threat is looming not just over the Western states, but that extends beyond our borders to the entire system. HUMINT suggests a growing network of individuals with ties to organized crime and potential terrorist affiliations."

"I suspect you want to see for yourself what happened to your officer. I'm sure you understand that due to the sensitivity of what I'm about to show you, we could not let this be uploaded to the shared network and be leaked to the news. We cannot afford the tech to double encrypt our files here with the federal budget we are given. Whomever this group is that we are dealing with, they are playing their cards close to their chest. Have they not made any declarations?"

Cohen said, "No. They accessed the UJS defense network via Belter tech."

"What? Did the Belt say anything about this, yet?"

"Not officially. Internally, they are running an internal investigation for a leak, but we haven't released this information to the public. So far, we know that it isn't an *official* Belter act. At least, that's what they're saying," Cohen responded.

"I mean, why would they? We're just now at a place where tensions are easing and it would be reckless to start another conflict on multiple fronts," Petrov said. "Their economy has been in decline the last few years and from the DIA reports, a not-so-modest percentage of their GNP goes to feeding their defense budget."

"That's what we're trying to figure out. War is often good for manufacturing and the domestic economy," commented Cohen.

Petrov responded, "Their economy has never been their strong suit. Their military prowess is."

Harper leaned back into the chair. "If whoever acted has the funding for Belter tech, that would mean they could have accessed anything we have sent. It's been well established in Tharsis that the Belt has exceptional SIGINT," said Harper.

"Callisto as it is has a hard enough time getting foot traffic," Ambassador Petrov said. "And a leaked incident like this would only exacerbate the situation. If you would be able to help encourage more federal relief our way, that would mean a world's difference."

"No promises, but I can see what we can do." Cohen took a sip of the Navy coffee. Still not the best, but he's had worse and tried to make the most of it.

Harper continued, "We understand there was a fatality. INTERPOL is taking this very seriously, which is why Cohen and I were chartered an express flight."

Petrov hesitated and muttered, "Why don't I just show you the CCTV footage." The ambassador turned her chair around and pressed a button on her mechanical keyboard. The semi-transparent projected monitor began to play a video.

The footage showed a bustling port hummed with activity as people shuffled towards the docking station, eager to board the waiting ship. A crowd moved towards the berth of the vessel. The chatter of frenzied conversations, the shuffling of feet, and the distant working of giant metal gears created a very busy environment. As the crowd neared the berth, a mustached man stood back and pulled out his personal terminal near a dark canal of water. He held his terminal to his ear and began speaking. The security footage was very clear but without any sound.

The crowd moved forward. As the man held back and continued to speak into the terminal.

"Watch here." Petrov pointed to the bottom of the screen.

From the depths of the water beneath the berth, a dark hand emerged and grabbed the ankles of the man. The hand yanked him downwards. His head slammed hard against the ledge. The hand continued pulling him beneath the surface. The crowd boarded the ship without notice of the action. The water bubbled briefly, then settled into stillness.

13

BLOOD SLOWLY DRIPPED FROM THE CEILING.

Maria cursed to herself as she gawked up at the ceiling and wall. It was barely 7 AM on a Tuesday morning in New London.

Maria Ramirez of the Ganymede Republic's Special Intelligence Service was assigned to this nightmare. She suspected it was likely a rookie hazing. As the young officer investigated the gruesome scene of shredded meat and metal, it took everything in here to keep her breakfast down. Although at the Academy she had been exposed to cadavers and the most grim footage someone could imagine, the type that would make the most abhorrent horror fan squeamish, seeing it in person was a whole other monster.

Ramirez had been assigned to a domestic terrorism case out of Derry that had led her into UJS territory to follow her lead. She had already been working the case this morning for three hours while on transit from The Castrum in Derry, Ganymede Republic.

Maria Ramirez had been burning the midnight oil when she had been assigned this case last night. With how time sensitive missing person cases were, her superiors at the SIS were able to accelerate her processing and permission to enter the UJS.

Maria Ramirez had been investigating the Ganymede First activist group as a potential terrorist organization. A journalist who had been critical of Ganymede First went missing last night. .

Upon arrival, Ramirez and the New London forensic team conducted a preliminary assessment of the train station's exterior. This involved observing the surroundings, access points, and any potential points of entry or exit. The security cameras were all fried with what appeared to be EMT pulses.

The position of the victim was documented with precise measurements and photographs. Ramirez bent down next to the young woman's body while another officer inspected. The forensics officer, Takashi Toriyama, noted the specific location, patterns, and quantity of the blood, including any apparent splatters, drips, or pooling.

Ramirez stood up and took off her gloves.

Takashi Toriyama continued to work on the corpse as he spoke to Ramirez. "We'll need to consult with our bloodstain pattern analyst to interpret the observed patterns. Standard protocol with blunt force trauma. Ain't much left of her. Our department's specialist was in Kepler City during the, uh...

well, we are having someone come in from Roosevelt to handle this in the interim until the department is back to full capacity. Need 'em to identify the splatter. Cap says she should be here by lunch. But you know how that goes."

Ramirez ran through her notes. She scrolled on her terminal to a photo of the missing journalist and held it up to compare it to one of the bodies on the floor. "With the damage to the face, I can't quite identify the body. The description matches her but ... fuck. Who could do this to someone?"

"Ah, this ain't nothin'. You should've seen the case last week in Reno. It was *way* worse. I'm talking full out bags of..."

"I'm good. Please stop."

"Sorry." Toriyama apologized as he began to pack away his samples. "You know, I don't think this was petty crime."

"Because they targeted the cameras first," she completed the thought.

"Yup. This had to be planned and EMT chargers ain't exactly *street legal*. Mafia don't hit like this, either. If they want you to disappear, you disappear without a trace. Usually out the wrong end of an airlock, or fed to the recyclers, or some shit. I've seen a lot of scenes. I'm pretty confident this was meant to deliver a message." The small man frowned. That's how she thought of him.

"What do you think the message is?"

"That's for you to find out. I'm just here to tell you what the leftovers are," Toriyama said. His expression returned to his cheery demeanor.

"Hmmm. When will you know if your Jane Doe is my girl?"

Ramirez' eyes were glued to the Rorschach painting of deep red across the tracks. A hell of a way to start the day.

"Well, we will need a thorough analysis to confirm the identity. We've created a comprehensive record of the crime scene so far. Once the splatter analyst gets here, we'll know more. After that, we'll transport the body to the lab for a more detailed analysis. The usual drill: post mortem examination, DNA testing, fingerprint analysis, yada yada yada. Just another day in paradise, am I right?"

He grinned and nudged Ramirez who was visibly shaken. He followed up, "It'll be alright. We'll find out if this is your girl."

She didn't say anything.

"First time seeing a fresh body?"

"I mean... I've seen dead bodies before. Just not like this."

Toriyama snapped up his case. "You'll get used to it. All part of the job, kid."

14

Viktor Kessler dictated to Michael Walker as he scribed on a tablet.

"Exhibiting an increase in bone density and skeletal muscle hypertrophy, imbalance in the amygdala has led to an extreme increase in testosterone levels and aggression. The correlation between psychopathy and aggressive behavior is specifically linked to a high ratio of testosterone to cortisol levels. We have effectively optimized maximum levels of aggression while minimizing inhibitory factors among the test subjects."

Walker's stomach growled softly. These shifts seemed to be getting longer and longer, and it was taking a toll on his wiry body. He could see new stress lines forming around his mouth when he shaved in the morning. Kessler admired his own reflection and straightened his tie before returning his focus to the agitated monster thrashing about behind the reinforced cage.

The cage was erected with high-strength alloys of stainless steel and aluminum, chosen for durability and resistance to corrosion. Advanced bonding techniques had been used to increase strength of the metal. Separating the gridded metal from the good doctor was a thick observation glass with large streaks of smudge marks.

The figure paced back and forth behind the glass, locking eyes with Kessler. He continued, "Enhanced security, military capabilities; the practical applications are limitless. I have engineered primal hostility on demand."

It snarled. Heat from its mouth briefly fogged a small part of the glass separating them. Kessler took off his thick rimmed glasses. He pulled out a microfiber handkerchief from his pocket. Kessler breathed on the lenses and wiped them with the handkerchief. The good doctor adjusted the spectacles on his face and stepped closer to the reinforced cage. He wanted a better view of his new friend. It slammed against the glass. Walker was startled by this and dropped his tablet and stylus pen. Mercer covered her mouth as she quietly laughed at Walker's reaction. Spit and blood smeared across the glass. Kessler smiled.

"Welcome to the future of controlled aggression."

15

THE UJS ARMED FORCES WERE STILL SEARCHING FOR WHO WAS responsible for the attack on Kepler City, which resulted in the death of over 3000 Jovian citizens. The Defense Intelligence Agency of the UJS had been investigating the trafficking of an upcoming weapon of mass destruction, likely a dirty bomb or some other atomic weapon. To have access to the necessary materials for an atomic weapon, all you need is the right tech and access to uranium, which is plentiful in the rocks of the Asteroid Belt. The problem was that the only two parties this far from the Sun that are known to have atomic tech are the Belt and the United Jovian System. Atomics were utilized for many things, but were forbidden by international law for manufacturing or production of weaponry.

In partnership with the Ganymede Republic's Special Intelligence Service, the UJS Defense Intelligence Agency had received confirmation that the Vanguard Solutions research center on Callisto is where their next weapon was being developed. With little government oversight in the protectorate of North Callisto, it was easy for an organization to remain in the dark. The blitz on Kepler City was a successful Hail Mary attempt and likely only possible due to the element of surprise.

The government began taking footage from a surveillance satellite of the facility to determine the best way to infiltrate. Based on the information sent by the late Clark Andrews, the facility was heavily guarded and in hostile territory. It would have been preferable to retrieve body cam footage from Andrews helmet, but his remains have still not been found. Due to the sensitive nature of his operation, he did not have his mission synced up to any back-up server.

The UJS had to rely heavily on the SIS' black operation to gather intelligence. The information retrieved and sent from Andrews confirmed this was the location of WILLOW and that Yuri Volkov was presently overseeing the project. During the surveillance, they observed the research facility to learn every detail. Despite this surveillance, they were never able to capture any footage of materials leaving the facility, Volkov, or any other high value target.

The President was briefed on the details of the mission titled Operation NIGHTFALL. The reliability of information obtained by spies in the field can vary widely and is influenced by numerous factors. Intentional deception, and the fluid nature of intelligence landscapes further contribute to the complexity of assessing the reliability of field intelligence. It is paramount for intelligence agencies to critically evaluate and corroborate information from multiple sources by cross-referencing to enhance accuracy and trustworthiness. If Operation NIGHTFALL went sour, it could result in the deaths of many Jovian commandos. If any of those Marines were captured and interrogated, they could potentially reveal classified and sensitive information. The President's advisors and his trusted cabinet members were skeptical of the operation. Motivated by the recent attack on Kepler City, the President decided to move ahead with the raid.

In the United Jovian System Armed Forces, the Marines are functionally the army of the Navy. In comparison to the Navy, the Marine Corps are a small, mobile, and specialized strike force. This delicate mission was assigned to a sheep dipped SOG called Spectre Team Four. This particular team is known for their expertise in special reconnaissance and extraction.

Spectre teams operate entirely in classified operations, (often black operations that *officially* never happened). The Spectre Training Program (SPECTRAP) is an 18-month program that is notorious for its rigorous selection process with a dropout rate of 95%. The program is designed to weed out candidates who cannot meet its demanding physical and mental standards. Fatalities have even occurred during SPECTRAP due to the extreme nature of the training exercises. Thanks to this refinement process, Spectres are the best of the best. Spectre Team 4 is organized into two color coded assault teams: Black and Red. Spectre Team 4 Red was assigned to NIGHTFALL.

The team was briefed on the mission to infiltrate the facility and capture Yuri Volkov. The *official* policy of the UJS was to never kill an enemy who has already surrendered, but it was rarely enforced. Based on the previous record of Volkov with the Ganymedean revolution, it was unlikely that he would surrender.

There had been many strategies derived for this particular extraction. UJS *could* alert the Belt of Volkov's presence. It was unknown, or rather unconfirmed at this time, whether or not Volkov was working as a rogue actor. He could be acting independently for the interests of the Belt. UJS and Ganymede Republic were working in tandem temporarily to eliminate this threat. Despite Olympus being claimed by both countries, and currently occupied by UJS, it was in their combined best interest to protect the people of Ganymede. Olympus was of no good to anyone if it laid in ruins or its people massacred.

Launching a ballistic projectile directly from Ganymede to the facility would draw too much attention. Likewise, if one were to grab one of the several meter wide rocks in Jupiter's rings and sling it towards the moon, it would suffer an even worse fate. Pinpointing the exact target trajectory to land on the precise coordinates had too many unreliable variables between orbiting bodies. Either scenario would flag every alarm and trigger system-wide panic. Another option considered was an air strike of the facility with stealth bombers. Any of these options would atomize Volkov and the weapon they were developing. The problem with this method is that they wanted to verify that Yuri Volkov was captured or at minimum, neutralized, and that the weapon was no longer a threat. Volkov had managed to escape military operations before. SecDef had described him as "very sneaky." It was learned the hard way that he used body doubles. A handful of *would be* assassinations resulted in the fatality of the wrong man with a striking verisimilitude.

Due to these factors, this operation was decidedly old school: violence of action. Boots on the ground for shock & awe (kicking in doors and aggressive insertion with an over-whelming force). The seasoned commandos of Spectre Team Four were flown in using modified helicopters. These were designed for stealth and the heat signatures or physical presence of the aircraft did not trigger radar.

In the early days of space exploration, scientists were not quite sure if it were even possible to pilot a helicopter in extra terrestrial environments. NASA's Mars Helicopter, *Ingenuity*, demonstrated successful flight on Mars in 2021 CE, showcasing the feasibility of controlled aerial mobility in the thin Martian atmosphere. Future missions leveraged the lessons learned from such endeavors to enhance the capabilities of aerial vehicles on the Red Planet.

All of the Galilean moons offer unique environmental conditions for flight, including their thin atmosphere, low gravity, extreme cold, and radiation exposure. The CO_2-based atmosphere is so thin and so faint on Callisto that it barely even exists at all. Helicopters on Ganymede and Callisto required significant modifications to adapt to the hostile terrain.

The SecDef received confirmation from the President of the United Jovian System, and directed the Admiral overseeing NIGHTFALL to move forward. Over the next few hours, the President and the national security team would watch the entire event unfold via the Situation Room in Roosevelt. His company in the Situation Room for this particular operation included the Vice President, the Deputy National Security Advisor, the Secretary of State, the Secretary of Defense, the Director of Defense Intelligence (Danielle Freeman), and various leaders of MARCOM. The entire event would be transmitted via body security cams and double encrypted. The Situation Room would see everything on a 4 second delay due to the sheer distance between Callisto and Ganymede.

The 12 commandos of Spectre Team Four had been temporarily transferred under the direct control of the Defense Intelligence Agency. This allowed the mission to move forward without the approval of the Jovian legislative branch. Since it *technically* is not a military mission as the DIA is a civilian agency, it is *technically* not illegal. Otherwise, they would need to seek approval from the Governor of North Callisto and the Jovian bicameral legislative branch. Due to the sensitivity and time constraint of NIGHTFALL, it would be far too risky for that information to leak. An information leak would result in the moving of the weapon and all high profile personnel before the mission could act. It is one of the most stressful and critically important missions in Jovian history.

Around 3 AM U.T.C., two helicopters descended near the research facility. The facility was 3700 square meters and 4 stories tall in the rim of a crater, with additional stories carved beneath the surface. An orbiting satellite scanned through the building with radar and infrared imaging that senses heat to estimate the opposition body count to prepare accordingly.

Two other helicopters hovered in formation nearby in case they were needed. The first helicopter hovered over the ground and deployed ropes to lower its teams to the surface of the moon. The other helicopter flew to the Northeast corner to deliver its remaining Marines. Albeit the two stealth helicopters were not detected or met with opposition fire, the delivery of Spectre was not without friction. The first helicopter flew into a vortex ring state before any Marines could deploy. This is a dangerous aerodynamic phenomena observed in helicopter flight where the rotor becomes engulfed in its own vortex ring system, resulting in a significant loss of lift. The phenomenon is often induced by temperatures exceeding initial projections.

The helicopter's rotor air pressure failed to dissipate effectively and grinded against the back of the compound wall. The tail rotor was seriously damaged and the helicopter began to tumble. The pilot nose-dived the helicopter into the Callisto regolith, thankfully preventing catastrophe. The Spectres inside the vehicle were able to deploy on the ground without any serious injuries.

Despite an absurd landing, this had not blown their mission. There were no alarms or signs of aggression from the facility. The other half of the team had landed safely on the Northeast corner. Each helicopter was equipped with a designated sniper. Each one was positioned at elevated vantage points located on opposing corners for a full view of the compound. At least what parts of the compound that weren't hidden in the crater rim mountains.

Each Marine Spectre wore a light-weight and slim fit tactical EVA suit called the Aspis Mark II. This suit was not designed for deep space vacuum, but for combat in thin atmospheres and pressurized environments. The armor featured strengthened joints, rendering it tear-resistant and impervious to bullets, within reason. Armor piercing ballistics and point-blank shots didn't hold up after consistent strain.

After scaling walls on opposing ends, the remaining members of Spectre Team Four reunited.

The next stage of the mission would be infiltrating the interior of the compound. This was the demolition team's time to shine. Their primary objective was shock and awe. Get in quickly, disrupt via chaos, grab their man, find the weapon, and get gone. Weeks had been spent preparing for this important mission. Once they were in the facility, every single second mattered.

In preparation, the team had assessed the compound's vulnerabilities and selected the entry point of the side air-lock. The Intelligence and Security Command had calculated the precise amount of explosive material needed to create a controlled breach without causing excessive damage. Proper coordination and precision are paramount to minimize collateral damage and maintain the element of surprise. The demolition team prepared the surface by ensuring it is clean and free from obstacles that might interfere. The duo applied the detonation cord, or det cord, to the airlock's locking mechanism and hinges. One of them secured the det cord in place using adhesive tape and attached a blasting cap, or detonator, to one end. This device was connected to a firing system that allows for remote initiation. On cue, the 12 Marines took cover on the adjacent walls of the airlock.

"Red Four-One, breaching airlock. Over," he said on the secure frequency.

"Four-One, this is Four-Actual. Send it. Over."

Red Six counted down with his fingers despite being in the near vacuum of Callisto's atmosphere. The call sign "Six" in a special operations group refers to the unit's commanding officer. The Six for Spectre Team Four - Red was Lieutenant Commander Kyle Woods. Even if he counted verbally, no one could hear what he was saying unless they were on the same radio frequency. They were trained a specific way and that discipline was followed whether in a pressurized environment or in the harsh vacuum of space. Discipline matters the most in less-than-ideal circumstances.

Red Six silently mouthed along as he mimed with his fingers 3, 2, 1. The demolition expert triggered the det cord.

After breaching the outer door, they were able to enter the airlock compartment. One of the commandos was able to force an automatic entry via a code-transmitter that overrode the 60 second pressurization cycle. This hack simultaneously disabled alarm notifications and kept life-support recovery systems online. It was a complicated little virus.

The first room past the airlock immediately dropped in air pressure as Spectre Team Four filed in.

"Four-One copies. Airlock breached. Pressure drop in first room. Sweeping now. Over."

As they rushed in, they first aimed at the corners and behind doors.

"Four-Two, left side clear," called a Marine at one end of the room.

"Four-Three, right side clear."

"Four-One to Four-Actual. Room one secure. Proceeding to next objective. Over."

"Four-Actual copies. Continue mission, out."

As the airlock door closed and sealed, the room they were in began to regain pressure immediately. All habitats had auto-pressurization systems in place for emergency breaches, such as a rogue meteorite the size of a raisin hitting the outer hull and causing a rapid decrease in pressure. It was rare, but it happened. Regardless, it is better to have the emergency system and not need it, than to need it and not have it. Like all things in the Jovian frontier, this lesson was learned the hard way through an extensive and well documented history of human tragedies.

The sound returned to the room as it repressurized. The screaming alarm was constant. After 20 seconds, Red Six received a notification on his HUD inside his helmet that the pressurization was back to normal. They kept their EVA combat fatigues on, but moving from room to room wouldn't cause massive drops in pressure. If pressurization was constantly changing, things got tricky. People passed out easier and died a lot easier, too. They needed Volkov alive. If they played their cards right.

The Aspis Mark II tactical helmet provided an independently sealed head module that covered most of their faces, with a wide visor allowing for maximal peripheral vision. One of the issues with full-face visors or glass-faced helmets was if the user bled or sneezed, it would disrupt their vision. They'd be functionally useless until they get the helmet off to clean it. In combat settings, the nose and mouth were protected. This was another one learned the hard way. Their helmets were covered with a dark threaded hexagonal net to reduce shine and break up the shape of the helmet, which made them a hard target for headshots.

Each commando's primary weapon was equipped with a Laika KH-13 6.5 mm semi-automatic rifle with extended magazine capacity. Laika, Inc. specifically built this model for the United Jovian Marine Corp. This gun was outfitted with a targeting laser, a short barrel, a muzzle brake, was optimized for high-velocity firing, and utilized 6.5 mm armor-piercing tungsten bullets. The weapon was made from good ole fashioned Jovian titanium and carbon fiber.

"Red Six to all call signs. Push forward. I say again, push forward. Over." commanded the Six on the in-ear comm system.

A Spectre turned and cracked open the next door to the hall with his foot. In his hand, he yanked the pin from the pineapple. The Marine's voice cracked as he screamed, "Frag out!" and tossed the grenade into the hall while closing the door. The commando, who affectionately called grenades *freedom nuggets*, turned to the wall next to the closed door and ducked. A loud explosion crashed in the next room as the door they were crouched beside shook.

The Marines breached through the settling smoke of the narrow hallway to find a warm body laying motionless against the wall. Another limp body was dangling half-way into the ceiling panel above them.

The counter terrorism task force turned and marched up the stairs of the compound. The first room they had entered on the second floor contained two adult personnel, but neither were Yuri Volkov. The two immediately threw their hands up in the air while collapsing onto their knees. They surrendered and were contained.

Even more unsettling, there were small groups of unattended children in medical gowns on each floor.

The events that happened next have varying descriptions from differing after-action reports. As the team got to the third floor, they faced even more opposition. They found Volkov's right-hand man, Moshe van Kerkywk. Spectre Luke White would later write a controversial book on the raid. White said van Kerkwyk was armed and shot at the Spectres. One Spectre suffered a minor injury. They returned fire and killed the courier. Some intel sources say otherwise, claiming the Spectres caught the courier off guard after cutting the lights. It was also reported that they eliminated him without a single shot fired at the Spectres.

Four minutes after the initial breach of the outer airlock, the resistance increased as they progressed into the facility. All enemies so far had either been killed or captured. The commandos climbed another set of stairs. They were shot at by another operator. The Spectre ducked and called out on the radio, "Contact left! Contact left! Taking fire! I repeat: taking fire!"

"Six to Two-One. Give me a SITREP. Over," responded Red Six on the radio.

"Charlie Fox. Shit!" he yelled as the bullets sprayed over his head. Tiny impact craters blasted into the stairwell wall adjacent to the wall the combatant was using for cover. "This is Two-One. Small arms fire from eleven o'clock. 10 meters out."

The enemy opp stood prepared around a corner with a 5.56×45mm Rockwell SL15 rifle stock tucked firmly into his shoulder. The terrorist wore a double reinforced armored vest, (bullet resistant and tear resistant, not bulletproof or inde-structible). He watched for the first visible reappearance of the Spectre's helmet above the final step. The commando collapsed. Blood had splattered against his shattered visor.

As the succeeding Spectres snaked up the stairwell, their new friend underhand tossed a grenade that bounced down-wards around the corners by their feet. The Marines dove for what little cover they could muster in the split second. There were worse ways to go, but not many.

The enemy opp had put down four of Spectre Team Four in less than 10 seconds.

Red Six clicked his rifle into a three round burst mode. He waited until the threat emptied their magazine. Red Six emerged from cover to shoot the terrorist with a flurry of hot metal. The bullets struck the combatant twice in the chest and once in the arm. A boyish yelp was followed by a curse. An armored vest may stop a bullet from penetrating, but the impact still hurts like hell and has been known to break a few bones. After a few more seconds, Red Six signaled for the team to move forward up the stairs. They checked the adjacent corners first. He escaped. The only remaining sign of the enemy was a few blood droplets floating in the air drifting to the ground. The assailant would later be identified as Nikolai Yurovich Volkov, son of the infamous Yuri Volkov.

The team was on the final floor of the compound to be

breached. The Spectres braced themselves for yet another letdown. This facility was a hot ticket item for the enemies of the United Jovian System. Despite being wanted for over five years, Yuri Volkov had a notorious reputation of being sly. He seemed to always be one step ahead of Ganymede's intelligence agencies.

The remaining commandos entered a room with an unarmed Yuri Volkov. He already had on his leggings and was wearing his communication cap snugly over his ears. He was in the middle of putting on the skin suit for his EVA suit to make his escape.

The demolition expert was the first to spot him. He did not miss a beat. "Four-One to all stations this net: Tango spotted! Office entrance, West side. Engaging target. Over."

The Spectre immediately fired at Volkov's legs in an attempt to slow him down. Yuri Volkov pulled the skinsuit above to his waist and stumbled back into his office.

The office contained several women. A woman in an officer's uniform charged at the commandos. The demolition expert shot her above her eyebrows and kept moving towards the office. She hit the ground like a bag of bricks. Red spilled from her face in rhythmic spurts as her heart kept beating in its final throes. The body twitched in a cadaveric spasm. The Marine who pulled the trigger would lose sleep over the memory for years to come.

"Four-One to all units: Multiple civilians in target location. One hostile, officer uniform. Neutralized. Continuing to objective. Over."

"Six copies. Confirmed hostile? Over."

"Four-One: Affirmative. Hostile charged position. Threat eliminated. No other resistance. Proceeding to secure Target. Over."

Yuri Volkov was trapped with the United Jovian System's most adept soldiers outside the room. Spectre Team Four had to play this carefully. The terrorist was one step away from hell. He now had a clipped wing from the previous burst and it was beginning to leak.

"Six to all units: Acknowledge last. Secure civilians. Four-One, continue pursuit. Four-Two, Four-Three, containment positions. Over."

"Four-Two: Roger. Moving to secure civilians."

"Four-One: Pushing to office. Stand by for contact. Out."

As the team crept through the door-way, Volkov grabbed a woman. The terrorist threw her at the Marines. They cast her aside to the ground. Volkov then sna tched another woman officer as a human shield. She squealed.

The Spectres ripped her out of his grips and tossed her aside. A Marine kicked the bleeding Volkov square in the torso, knocking him onto the floor.

As Volkov began to move, a Marine fired three rounds to the right of his head and he stopped. Red Six told Four-One to hold position.

Red Six radioed the REMFs in the Situation Room. He said, "Six to Overlord: Red Four-Actual. Target acquired. Awaiting further instructions. How copy? Over."

·　·　·

"Overlord to Red Four-Actual. Solid copy all day. RTB. Over," said the command duty officer. She grinned and relaxed in her seat. Dopamine rushed through her body from an exhilarating mission.

An inaudible message came to Callisto. Likely interference due to the ever changing trajectories and orbits of the moons around Jupiter.

Red Six clarified, "Do not copy. Repeat?"

Overlord repeated the transmission.

"Red Four-Actual copies. Standing by, target secured. Roger that RTB. Out."

" ," announced the President with a heart-felt fist pump. Cheers erupted in the Situation Room in Roosevelt.

This was a major victory for the United Jovian System against the terrorists who attacked Kepler City. This may be their first, but not their last.

Volkov's hands were being tied behind his back while laying face down on the floor. He demanded, "What is this?"

The Marine tied the knot even tighter and replied, "Justice."

16

Spectre Team Four searched the room. They found a rifle and a pistol that were not loaded. Volkov had not been expecting such a rambunctious early morning.

Immediately after detaining the terrorist, a Marine pulled off his shemagh tactical scarf to place on the leaking hole in Yuri Volkov's limb. A few minutes later, the team Corpsman came from behind and grabbed his leg to examine the wound. He ripped Volkov's bloodied seams apart to expose the skin. It had a clean hole on both sides of his upper thigh. Thankfully, the hot lead missed the femoral artery. The Corpsman was rougher than usual, professionalism be damned. He applied direct pressure to the wound using a clean cloth and instructed another Marine to hold the cloth while he pulled out a combat application tourniquet from his medical kit. The Corpsman placed the tourniquet a round the injured limb, several inches above the wound. He pulled the tourniquet strap firmly into a snug fit. It was secured in place. The Marine pulled the strap through the ratcheting buckle and locked it.

He smeared a hemostatic agent directly to the hole to trigger blood clotting. The Corpsman stuck his thumb into the hole and squeezed against the side of the wound.

Volkov groaned.

"Stay still. I need to make sure the hole is clean," he lied. The Corpsman completed dressing the wound. He pulled out a cylindrical digital device and pressed it against the fresh blood on the ground. The device was a Rapid Response DNA Analyzer that confirmed the blood matched that of Yuri Volkov and not of *another* body-double. Once receiving the confirmation on his HUD, the Corpsman bounced the confirmation notification to the rest of the team's visors.

He pulled Volkov up to his feet. "Alright, you piece of shit. Let's go."

Three other Marines accompanied the Corpsman and Yuri Volkov out of the office. The lingering Spectres on the top floor remained calm and focused. The mission was not yet over. They would be extracting soon, but there was still housekeeping to tend to. Clark Andrews had confirmed that the research facility contained vital intelligence and evidence on Operation WILLOW.

Meanwhile, the team leader reported to the Situation Room while the Corpsman worked on the detained terrorist.

"Overlord, this is Team Four-Actual. Objective one accomplished. Target is prepared for extraction. Heading towards the helo. Proceeding to locate the second objective. Stand by for further intel."

"Team Four-Actual, this is Overlord. Message received. Proceed with caution. Over." The radio signal responded to every Spectres EVA helmet. The voice had the high mids tone of radio broadcasted frequency.

The team leader directed the remaining men. "Alright, boys. Alpha team, with me. Bravo team, search the library. Stay frosty."

The remaining men broke into their designated groups and spread out. Their steps were delicate. The Spectres' rifles were held high as they began searching the remaining rooms and halls.

"There's no one left," one Marine complained after searching a few empty rooms.

"Cut the chatter and stay focused on the mission," corrected Red Six.

"I'm tellin' you. There isn't anyone here," he bitched again.

"Martinez, you're going to get another *Page 11*," responded another Marine.

Red Six remained silent as he searched. The Spectre Team Four operators moved through the dimly lit corridors. They found a hydraulically sealed door as the team continued throughout the building. A Spectre disabled the security override and unlocked the door. Panels hissed and gears whined as the door mechanically opened. Cooled mist billowed out of the freezer like rolling fog. The Marines had breached the reinforced door and entered a high-tech laboratory. They walked by aisles of empty enclosed chambers and monitors. The room had an observation office attached to it, but the door was locked. A Marine shot the door lock, blowing the handle off. He pushed the door open.

Another Spectre approached a central console in the office. Cryptic data scrolled across high contrast screens. He typed a few keys and examined the console. The Spectre said, "We've got something. WILLOW. It's uh not a bomb."

"What is it?" Martinez asked from behind.

"Whatever it is. It's been activated."

Almost every enemy in the facility had been killed. The two that surrendered, Volkov, and his officer were detained in custody on one of the helicopters, seated in between the stacked bodies of the 4 deceased Marines. Three Spectres remained with the assumed hostages and children until the North Callistan forces arrived.

Mercer and Walker remained silent when they were shuttled into the transport during the evacuation from the research facility. Infiltration had always been prepared for. They knew for now they had to keep quiet and keep their heads to the ground.

The damaged helicopter was not in shape for departure. North Callisto's forces would be arriving soon. Although a protectorate of the UJS, they could not risk letting the helicopter fall into the wrong hands. It contained vital information to the advanced stealth technology and operations of the UJS armed forces. The risk of a leak of that information could not be permitted.

At 4 AM U.T.C., due to the confidential nature of the Spectre operation, the demolition team applied the same portable explosives that they used to breach the compound onto the inoperable aircraft. The helicopter erupted in a fiery fury. One Marine shot a flare gun skyward to signal their location to their back-up team. A bright flare seared into the thin air. Within a few minutes, a back-up helicopter arrived to extract the remaining Spectres.

17

"HOW WOULD THAT WORK?" SHE ASKED BEFORE BITING INTO A slice of pizza. It was too hot and burnt the roof of her mouth. This was her nightmare. Maria Ramirez was still in New London on a missing person case. Her body was shaped like an hourglass, if an hourglass was shaped like a barrel. The rookie had been paired with a local Jovian forensic detective named Takashi Toriyama since the morning of the train accident.

"Alright," Toriyama continued as they walked down the busy street. "If someone were able to initiate nuclear fusion in Jupiter's core, it could reach critical mass and pressure similar to what happens in a star."

"What do you mean?"

"Well. Hydrogen is the most common element in the observable universe. Right?"

"Sure."

"Right. Jupiter is primarily composed of hydrogen and helium. These two elements make up more than 99% of the total mass of the planet. It's a gas giant, right? The outer atmosphere of the planet contains other shit like methane, water vapor, ammonia, some other compounds, but the vast majority of its mass is in the form of molecular hydrogen and helium." Toriyama finished his thin slice and wiped his beard with a napkin. He spoke elaborately with his hands as he described the planet.

"Okay. But what you're saying is it would be a star?"

"Yes! Jupiter was thought *initially* to be a protostar. I mean, compositionally, it shares a lot of similarities with stars. The Sun is also mostly hydrogen and a bit of helium. Jupiter just never had enough um, mass to initiate nuclear fusion in its core to become a full-fledged star."

"So in this hypothetical scenario, they would just turn Jupiter into a star? And that would destroy life as we know it?"

"Yeah. Pretty much. If someone could figure out how to trigger nuclear fusion in Jupiter's core. We're talkin' about an *extinction level event*. Think of it like this: Jupiter would become a Brown Dwarf. Bigger than a gas giant but smaller than your standard star. Right? The effects on the system would be profound, *probably* altering the dynamics of the orbits of nearby planets and other celestial bodies: asteroids, rocks, moons, and shit. This would likely lead to the extermination of... well, everything alive, at least."

"Yikes. Let's hope that never happens. Have you ever thought about teaching?"

"I *actually* used to teach, but the pay's shit. So now I just do this."

"New London PD must pay better than the SIS does. Our hours are long and the pay isn't much."

"Better than teachin' salary."

"Let me guess, you taught P.E.?"

"Funny! No. Chemistry, actually."

"Less stressful?" replied Ramirez sardonically.

"Yeah, actually. If you can imagine."

"Either way, I think you might have too much time on your hands."

As the two detectives turned around the corner, they saw a mass of protestors. The streets of New London were filled with angry people. The metropolitan district of New London was just East of Olympus in United Jovian System territory. Thousands of bodies swarmed the streets in front of where the Kepler City refugees were sheltered. Protestors shouted slogans and waved signs. The crowd was divided. There were those in jubilant celebration that Yuri Volkov was captured the day prior. Volkov was assumed to be the culprit of the attack on Kepler City. There were those who supported the cause of a free Olympus but not of the violence. Then there were those who viewed the attack on Kepler City as justified.

Maria Ramirez pushed through the throngs of angry protesters. It reminded her of pushing her way through a bustling concert crowd to the stand by the stage.

"This is ridiculous!" she complained.

Ramirez fought her way through the crowd with Toriyama.

A rock suddenly flew through the air. Ramirez was struck in the face. She staggered backward. A deep cut stung above her brow. A discombobulated Ramirez stumbled as she tried to regain composure.

"Everything is black."

"What?" shouted Toriyama. The crowd was getting louder. People were beginning to push.

"Everything is black!"

"Is that like a metaphor?" asked Toriyama. He caught up to Ramirez and saw the deep cut on her face. The detective pulled her off to the side of the mob.

"No, I genuinely can't see. That fuckin' rock must've broke my ocular implants. I can't see a god damned thing. That god damned piece of shit."

"Are you okay?"

"Yeah, my head hurts. Don't worry about me. I'll be fine." She felt around until she grabbed his arm. "Just in the dark until I can get them recalibrated by a tech." She heard a blood curdling scream. Then gun fire. The young detective felt a knot form in her stomach.

"Come on. We gotta get out of here!" Toriyama called out as he pulled her arm.

The crowd had turned into a riot. Local shop glass windows and doors began to break. The rioters surged like a whitewater rapid. They pushed and pulled. More gun fire. More screams. The noise of the terrified crowd grew louder as everyone tried to flee at once. Fists flew and began to claw past them. She gritted her teeth and pushed forward against the violence. Toriyama's grip on her arm tightened as he pulled her through the crowd.

"What is going on? I can't see anything," she shouted.

"These people are losing their minds! Watch out!" Toriyama shoved Ramirez down. A body was thrown to the ground right where they were just standing. The person on the street writhed in pain. An armored monster jumped on top of the person on the ground. It began to slash frantically at them as they curled into the fetal position.

"We need to leave. Now!" Toriyama pulled the blinded young detective over his shoulders in a fireman's carry as he began to run with the crowd as it scattered in every direction like a swarm of crawling insects.

More monsters jumped down on the people around them as they were being picked off one by one as Toriyama sprinted with Ramirez on his back.

Toriyama screamed as they were shoved from behind. The two tumbled to the ground and rolled. Ramirez called out for her partner. No response. All she heard was the sound of violence and panic all around her. The detective crawled up to her feet and began running in a direction. Any direction. Away from the noise.

Everything was black.

Due south of New London, there was a failed attack in Fallujah the same day. It was later discovered that the dropship carrying the monsters in New London was cleared for passage by an air traffic controller.

A career Navy Sailor named Adrian Meadows. Adrian's twin brother James was also a career Navy Sailor. The brothers had descended from a long line of Navy veterans. James happened to be on the naval air traffic team in Athens. He held the more senior title of Senior Officer of Operations at his post. The fact that James was *technically* born first by a few minutes, was 0.125 cm taller, *and* had a more senior title was a point of contention (not to mention frequent teasing) between the two. Adrian was stationed in New London. After the outbreak of WILLOW, Adrian sent a direct message to James that the dropship had gained security clearance for landing with a specific encrypted access key. This was the last time that James would ever communicate with Adrian.

Another freight dropship's radar pinged his operation point's computer within a few minutes. Radars for the UJS operated by pinging one another's radar transponder to collect data. This gave a more detailed breakdown about the vessel rather than an ambiguous blob on a radar screen. The ship gained clearance to land in Fallujah using the exact same encrypted access key as before. It was suspected the terrorists had planned the freight ships to drop at the same time to use the element of surprise and overwhelm each city.

Meadows did not have much time to react as the ship was already cleared for docking, to verify the identity of the incoming ship to confirm that it is a combatant and not an Jovian vessel being misrepresented, or to notify higher command authorities. Normally, the rules of engagement that governed interactions with threatening vessels would be carefully reviewed to determine the appropriate response in each scenario. Meadows did not have the luxury of time and had to react fast.

Adrian Meadows wasn't able to describe to James Meadows in immense detail what was going on in New London, but he made it clear that New London was under serious attack. The next 30 seconds would later result in a lengthy court martial and eventual acquittal. Meadows directed defensive action to prevent the potential release of the unknown weapon retroactively known to be WILLOW. The Missile Defense Officer verified the missile system was accurately tracking the target's movement. Meadows ordered the Fire Control Technician to fire on the seemingly benign civilian vessel. The Fire Control Technician refused and was immediately relieved of duty. Meadows ordered the Missile Systems Officer to fire two high-explosive warheads at the freighter. The officer obeyed. The dropship carrying a payload of monsters was neutralized.

Leadership at the DIA realized that there must be collusion between compromised individuals within Jovian agencies. The only ways to have gained that specific access key was through hacking or through someone within the Jovian defense community (whether military or a non-military intelligence agency). Someone may have leaked information to the enemy.

18

"Let's cut the bullshit. What the hell happened yesterday?"

The President was surrounded by his most trusted advisors, national security staff, and high ranking government officials. The conference room was as packed as a jar of pickles. The walls were lined with chairs seated with top national security officials. At the center of the room was a bona fide Earth-grown North American Oakwood table. Seated at the table were the President, the Vice President, the National Security Advisor, the Secretary of Defense, the Secretary of State, the Director of Defense Intelligence (DDI), the Deputy Director of Operations (Intelligence), and the lead Analytics and Field Operations (Intelligence) Officer.

The room remained silent. All eyes on the President, waiting for his reaction.

Naomi Asimov, the Secretary of Defense, spoke up. "It was

a god damn nightmare, sir. Yuri Volkov and his friends released these monsters in New London. News outlets are calling them *reapers.* There was chaos in the streets. We're still piecing together the full extent of the damage."

Director of Intelligence Danielle Freeman spoke up. "We've got Yuri Volkov en route from North Callisto. They're deciphering what all they found there. It's only a matter of time before we've got operating intel, sir. We know Yuri was involved. We *will know* who else is responsible."

The President leaned back in his chair. The stress from this term was making him noticeably older by the day.

"As soon as he sets foot on this moon, I want him in questioning. Find out what Yuri Volkov knows *by any means necessary.* Do I make myself clear?"

"Yes, sir," replied Dir. Freeman. "Our field op department has been investigating WILLOW under Officer Asher Cohen."

Asher Cohen coughed out of a few jitters. The Analytics and Field Operations Officer had never spoken directly to the President before. It was intimidating to have the undivided attention of the most powerful man in the system.

"I've been working on this opp for months, but here are the basics: the attack on Kepler City and New London were from a terrorist faction. What we are seeing is Operation WILLOW. A bioengineered weapon of mass destruction."

"Is it contagious?" asked Sec. Asimov.

Cohen said, "We don't know. Until two days ago, we suspected WILLOW was an atomic weapon."

"Whatever this is, it has decimated the population of New London," commented Secretary of State Cormac Keyes.

"It could have been worse."

Sec. Keyes continued, "If we can't contain this-"

"The breached city district is under quarantine. New London *is* contained," corrected Sec. Asimov. "Hell, we stopped them in Fallujah."

"Those dropships were neutralized before they could dock and release. Once these things are let loose-"

"Reapers."

"Excuse me. Once these *reapers* are let loose-"

"What are our options?" asked the President.

"We could send in armed forces to neutralize what's left of the occupying force."

"We need a calculated response," said another advisor.

"I don't know if you have seen any of the footage. Most of them are already dead. This would be mercy. These people are already suffering a fate worse than death," said a presidential aide.

The room fell silent for a beat.

"Do we have any other options?" asked the President.

"Sir, we could utilize orbital bombardment," proposed Sec. Asimov.

"What?" asked an aide.

"But that would kill thousands of people," said Sec. Keyes.

"Yes," replied Sec. Asimov.

"Absolutely not," said the President.

"That would demolish the entire district in New London.

There would be no chance of recovery after that," defended Sec. Keyes.

"What is the best way we can execute this?" asked the President. "I do not want to risk any more lives than necessary."

Sec. Asimov proposed a more pragmatic solution. This was followed by dead silence from the officials around the table. Those elected by the people to safeguard their welfare, commerce, and security.

An advisor remarked, "Say goodbye to your second term."

"I'm not *worried* about optics. I'm *worried* about our people suffering," said the President.

"You can't steer a ship if you're thrown overboard. You can't help anyone if you're not re-elected."

"If it means saving people, that's a chance I'm willing to take," the President concluded. "As for your proposal, I don't like it."

"You don't have to *like* it. This is the right thing to do," replied Sec. Asimov. She turned to the semi-transparent projected wall monitor and activated the live video feed from the New London CCTV network. This was a private network not available to the public. The footage showed the streets filled with people torn apart. Human bodies were scattered in pieces. The room was uncomfortably quiet.

"We need to continue exploring more direct options. For now, we will move forward in 12 hours," directed the President.

"Yes, sir."

Sec. Keyes rubbed his forehead with his hand. "History will not remember us kindly."

"Look at me." Sec. Asimov fought for eye contact with the Secretary of State. "Look. Look at me. There might not *be* a history if we can't protect the Jovian people. These people in New London are dead. We need to accept that. Our loyalty is to the people *alive* today, not what some arbitrary history books will have to say about this."

The President redirected the conversation, "Do we have anything actionable concerning who is behind this?"

"Not at this time, sir," replied DDI Freeman.

The President shifted in his chair. He rubbed his chin with his hand.

Cohen quietly spoke, "I have something."

"What was that?"

"I may have something," he said a little louder.

DDO Samuel Thornton, Asher Cohen's direct supervisor, tried to hush him before the President insisted he speak his mind.

"Based on the intel we received yesterday from the operation to retrieve Yuri Volkov from the Vanguard Solutions research facility on Callisto, we have learned that Vanguard Solutions is testing this bioweapon for the Belt on Jovian lives."

"Have we confirmed the Belt is behind this?" asked Sec. Keyes

"No. Not at this time. We have only confirmed that Vanguard Solutions is developing weapons *for* the Belt. Whether or not the Belt knows where this testing is being done, is not yet confirmed."

"It's irrelevant if they know or not. These are Jovian lives being lost," explained Sec. Asimov.

"Does Ganymede Republic know about this?" asked the President. His voice was calm, direct, and commanding.

"Nobody outside this room knows, sir."

"Vanguard Solutions is not acting alone."

"Vanguard Solutions. They also do R&D furium, don't they?" asked the Vice President.

"A subsidiary department does, yes."

"Who is their head of research?"

"Viktor Kessler -"

"Motherfucker," muttered an advisor.

"-is their Director of Advanced Research & Development. We are working on contacting him, sir," replied DDI Freeman.

"When you do, I want him detained immediately. Notify me as soon as he is found."

"Yes, sir."

"Our intel suggests this and the Kepler City attack were both Ganymede First," explained DDO Thornton.

"Is that confirmed?"

"No," replied DDI Freeman.

"Alright. We need actionable options based on confirmed information."

Cohen elaborated. "Ganymede First is an extremist faction of the GRPA. Almost all of their members are former GRPA, and UJS before that. Their mission statement is for a free and unified Ganymede, starting with the reunification of Olympus with the remaining West districts of the Ganymede Republic."

The Deputy Director of Operations continued where Cohen left off, "It has become apparent that since they cannot match our fire power, their efforts have been to destabilize the surrounding districts further until they become ungovernable."

Sec. Keyes stated, "Olympus is an integral part of the United Jovian System, its sovereignty and territorial integrity's protected under the principle of consent as outlined in the ceasefire agreement with the Western districts. Their status as part of the UJS is deeply ingrained in Jovian identity and history. This is non-negotiable. The potential destabilizing effects of ceding Olympus include violence, sectarian conflict, *and* the impact of our international standing *and* sure, security interests. Hell, the entire election pivoted on maintaining Olympus's position within the union. We have tried to seek peaceful resolutions to this conflict through negotiations and security measures. After this second attack, it is clear that force is *necessary* to neutralize this threat."

"We have a duty to protect the people of Ganymede," defended Vice President Andronici.

"They do not give a shit about *the people of Ganymede*," explained the frustrated SecDef.

"What we can confirm is that there is a highly organized and well-funded group with an agenda to make the Northern districts ungovernable," said DDI Freeman.

The President asked his most trusted advisors, "What do you think is the cause of this?"

The President was elected by the Parliamentary Congress in an aggressive campaign. The controversial election was referred to by talking heads as cutthroat. It had been very close, resulting in the aging incumbent replaced by a younger man with outstanding speaking skills, strong principles, and even stronger opinions. As an independent, he was able to unify the United Jovian System as one nation. Part of his charm was his willingness to see things from outside his perspective. The road to hell was paved with good intentions. Those good intentions often fail due to lack of perspective. His team of trusted aides and advisors were hired and appointed to see what he could not. He needed their perspective and advice even if he did not always follow it.

"Their aim is to exploit the existing tensions between UJS and the Ganymede Republic. They are using Olympus as a deliberate ploy and manipulating us to their advantage," replied DDI Freeman.

"What is their advantage in this?"

"Sir, The Castrum denies vehemently any involvement. We have a meeting with them immediately after this. They were instrumental in the discovery of Operation WILLOW's location on Callisto," replied DDI Freeman.

"At this time, they are not a direct threat," assessed Sec. Asimov.

"The WILLOW weapon has been built. New London is just the first wave. If the Belt gets their hands on this tech-" said DDI Freeman.

"We are not at war with the Belt," corrected Sec. Keyes.

"What do you know about this Ganymede First group?" asked the President.

"They're terrorists closely tied to Yuri Volkov and Anton Krasnyy," explained Cohen.

"When was the last time we heard from Krasnyy?" asked Sec. Keyes.

"Officially? Five years ago. We have documented appearances in Derry since then, but nothing we can act on. It's outside our jurisdiction," explained Sec. Asimov.

"It's only illegal from an operational perspective and only if we get caught," commented an advisor.

"Absolutely not." The President immediately shut down that idea. "This happened because the West doesn't trust us. The last thing we need right now is to betray their trust when they are willing to help."

"Anton Krasnyy and Yuri Volkov *are* Belters, not Ganymedeans," said Sec. Asimov.

"Neither have worked directly for the Belt since before the war," explained DDI Freeman, referring to the revolutionary war of the Ganymede Republic.

"Do not underestimate the Belt. Yuri Volkov and Anton Krasnyy are puppeteers caught between two worlds," snapped back Sec. Asimov.

"At this time, the Belt is continuing to cooperate. What we can confirm is that Krasnyy and Volkov are acting *independently* of the Belt. These attacks are not state sanctioned," said Vice President Adronici.

"We've confirmed the use of Belter tech to hijack the Rod from God on Kepler City," explained Cohen.

"Yes. What we *can* confirm is that they have access to Belter tech. Not that the Belters gave them the tech," said Sec. Asimov.

"Fuckin' rock monkeys," someone remarked.

The group ignored the slur.

"Sir, what we *do know* is that a terrorist organization is behind this. This is not a state-sanctioned attack by the Ganymede Republic or the Belter Empire. Vanguard Solutions developed WILLOW and is testing it against Jovian citizens. A terrorist organization used it. It is suspected to be Ganymede First as their close proximity to Anton Krasnyy and Yuri Volkov. We do not know why," clarified Cohen.

The President kept everyone focused, "Keep me updated once you've verified the information. Until then, we need to seek other direct actions."

"Yes, sir," said the Secretary of Defense.

"Thank you, Sec. Asimov and Mr. Cohen."

Cohen responded with heartfelt sincerity. "Thank you, Mr. President."

19

In a dimly lit coffee shop tucked away in a quiet corner of Derry, Luis Hernandez sat at a secluded booth next to a Polybius arcade machine. The man tapped his foot nervously against the tiled floor while watching the entrance. A large man in a sharp suit entered. Hernandez slid out of his booth and approached the Deputy Director of Operations, their meeting appeared as nothing more than two old friends catching up in the bustling Black Gold Cafe.

Thornton placed his terminal visibly on the table to record the conversation. It was not connected to any remote networks or cloud databases to prevent any foreign interception of information. If something were to happen to Thornton and his terminal, that information would be permanently lost. It was a risk they were more than willing to take to ensure privacy of delicate information.

Thornton reached his hand out and rhetorically said, "So, you're Asher's friend."

Hernandez stood up and wiped his sweaty palms on his pants before he had his hand *crushed* by Thornton's vice grip of a handshake. Outwardly, he returned the firm shake with all his might. Intelligence agencies were still an old boys' clubs and a macho facade was often performed as a power play. He was squirming inside from the pain in his hand.

"Not quite, but we have a mutual acquaintance."

"I'm Sam Thornton." Some folks have voices that are smooth as butter. Thornton's wasn't.

"I know. My name is Luis Hernandez. I'm sorry about what happened in New London. I can only imagine how-" He wasn't cut off, but Hernandez lingered. He didn't complete the sentence. Speaking it aloud somehow made it worse. It wasn't too long ago that these two were enemies, and their respective countries didn't necessarily see eye to eye on sensible issues of governance.

Thornton took off his jacket. They both sat opposite in the secluded booth. He reassured, "Alright. Things are tense right now. I don't have much time. What else do you have for me?"

This relaxed Hernandez a bit. "A few weeks ago, we captured someone involved with a bombing on our side of the curtain. As a gesture of our commitment to peace, we want to give him to you."

"And how can we be sure this isn't just another trick?"

Hernandez leaned forward, no longer relaxed. "Because we want to end the violence as much as you do."

"Funny way of showin' it."

"We're not responsible for the attacks. Those were rogue agents."

"Are they Provisional Army?"

"As far as we know."

"So a few rogue agents who happen to be a part of your organization?"

"Those men are terrorists. They are not acting on our orders. We've condemned their actions and we're continuing to offer our cooperation to ensure they face justice. We've been nothing but transparent this entire time. Our officer Elsie Harper has been working with your department. One of our best men died to get the information on Volkov to you."

"Is that so?" The information surrounding Clark Andrews' mission and missing person status were on a *need to know* basis. Thornton didn't need to know. He suspected the claim was bullshit intended to manipulate him.

Hernandez reassured, "Damn right it is."

"How convenient."

"I'm trying here." Hernandez held up his hands palms-out in front of his chest, as if surrendering. "It's better you take 'em off our hands and do what needs to be done."

Thornton took a deep breath and pressed his back further into the booth seat. "Where did you find him?"

"One of their insider grunts came to us and defected in exchange for full amnesty. He couldn't live with the guilt and told us all he knew. Didn't know much. Intel tracked the information given back to this *other* kid. Gotta be late teens. Some poor kid who got swept up in propaganda." Hernandez took a drink of his coffee, smacked his lips, and set the mug down. "That other kid, that's who I want you to take. He won't talk to us. But his network address was cited for hacking into the Jovian satellite that dropped *the rod* on Kepler City."

"Rookie mistake."

Hernandez agreed, "You're not wrong, but if these guys were sharp enough to not make any mistakes, they'd probably be reasonable enough not to be terrorists or try to blow themselves up just to prove something. I don't get it. I've spent time around these Ganymede First guys and they're not exactly valedictorians."

"It was only a few years ago that *Pugna Nostra* and the Ganymede Republic were considered terrorists. Some are convinced you people still are."

That kept Hernandez quiet for a beat at the backhand sting. He deflected, "All revolutionaries and freedom fighters are considered terrorists one way or another."

"I suppose so. Have you identified him yet?"

"No. He's not in any known database. The lease was under a fake name. No fingerprints and dental records line up. DNA don't sync up with anything, at least not from our database. The kid simply doesn't exist. Whoever he works for really did their homework."

"You said he hasn't said anything useful?"

"Not a peep. He hasn't said a single word."

After a brief pause, Thornton continued, "We'll take them into custody. But mark my words, if this is some sort of ploy-"

"It's not. We want peace as much as you do."

"How do you propose we get your man?"

"We deliver him to the border via a heavily guarded convoy."

"Is he a physical threat?"

"No, he's a string bean. *But,* he has friends in high places. We can take him wherever you want, or we can transfer custody immediately at the border."

"We'll take full custody at the border."

"Sounds good. When can we transfer the asset?"

"Tonight at midnight."

20

"Yes, sir. Understood," Chen parroted into the phone terminal. The Chief of the Watch was a stern middle-aged woman known for running a tight ship. A sprawling control module and support systems filled the monitors of the city's control center. Two technicians sat at nearby parallel stations in front of Chen.

She hung up the phone terminal and turned to a fledgling operator. Chen gave him the order.

"Sir, that protocol... We can't–"

Chen cut him off, "That's an order."

The operator did not say anything. Chen repeated the order.

He hesitated and responded, "No."

"What was that?"

"I ... can't ... I won't do it. No, sir."

"Okay. You're relieved of duty. Exit the deck immediately."

The junior operator paused, stood up, and walked out the command center. His coworker began to fidget in her seat. The Chief of the Watch gave the order to the second technician at the module. The young operator swallowed hard and moved her shaking hands to the console. Her fingers hovered over the keyboard.

"Yes, sir."

The only time the DIA worked abroad with foreign international intelligence agencies was when specifically invited to assist on a particular case by a foreign national. When the DIA was previously under Director Waldrum, there was a strict rule against exchanging information with the SIS. The SIS had refused to give the source of a whistleblower for a scandal within the DIA. That scandal was the public death of the fragile relationship between the SIS and the DIA. Waldrum was convinced it was due to some soft kid with conviction who couldn't keep a secret. Due to the integrity of the SIS to protect its sources, the goodwill between the two agencies eroded. If two officers from opposing agencies met to exchange information, they had to do so in a clandestine environ. As with all things, the old guard passed and the rules of the game changed. As the newest Director Freeman took her position in the DIA, she restored communication between the rival intelligence agencies, and trust had been slowly rebuilding. The DIA and SIS already started on rocky ground due to the secession of the Ganymede Republic from the United

Jovian System. Over the years, there had been some operations they had partnered with together, but they were few and far between. It wasn't perfect, but it was better. For every one step the DIA took, the Ganymede Republic had to take three to compensate.

The Ganymede Republic and United Jovian System territorial border was quiet at midnight. The desolate, rocky landscape was so small under a colossal Jupiter in the sky.

The DIA extraction team traveled in a pair of long-range special operations vehicles, painted in sand and gray camouflage that blended in with the tidally locked surface to keep a low profile. They rode in 4x4 reconnaissance jeeps equipped with enormous off-road rock climbing tires and ballistic armor exteriors. To travel by a bird required additional approval and Thornton was wanting to keep this as close to the chest as possible. There was a suspected leak somewhere in the department and the less people knew, the better.

"Still talking to her?" asked Deputy Director Samuel Thornton.

"Yeah." replied Asher Cohen who was admiring the horizon.

"You're going to have to move on."

"I know."

The jeep bounced across the rocky terrain and began a descent up from the valley of a crater.

Cohen *hated* silence. Even though he knew the answer, he still paged over a private comm link to Thornton, "So, we're picking him up at the border?"

"Yeah. SIS is handing him over at midnight."

Cohen sat in the back seat next to his mentor. Two security officers sat in parallel captain chairs in the front.

"Any update on who this punk is?"

The vehicle climbed over rocks and elevation changes over the barren terrain.

Thornton said, "Someone worth knowing. Convicted terrorist. Failed bombing attempt. We don't know the details. Yet."

"Maybe they were working in tandem with the suicide bomber we picked up. Has he said anything?"

"Not yet. Something big is in the works and he hasn't said a word." A tight smirk spread across Thornton's face. "Well. We'll get him to talk. We always do. Don't we?"

Cohen responded, "Seems to be your specialty, sir."

Could there really be something bigger planned than the attack on Kepler City? The DIA's perspective on interrogation was that whether it's sleep deprivation, reduced confinement, caloric restriction, or other more creative solutions, everyone eventually spilt the beans. Critics and academic nosebleeders said if you had the time, the most effective way to extract information from a detained asset would be to become their best friend. But the DIA didn't have much time to spare.

Blinking lights had been installed every 10 km on the lunar surface to indicate the border between the two countries. They had agreed to meet at coordinates ~ 50 km away from any major building. In the distance lights began to sparkle into existence as a helicopter descended, tossing lunar regolith briefly in the air.

The two groups separated from their vehicles once the dust had settled. The DIA team had to climb down out of the jeeps on retractable ladders. The bottom of the cabs stood over 3 meters tall from the ground. The vehicles did not have doors.

The parties approached from each side the closest glowing border marker. For prisoner exchanges, the number of personnel is kept to a minimum to maintain operational security. The DIA party was made of armed security personnel, two intelligence agency members, and a physician.

Across the border, Luis Hernandez, Jean-Luc Devis, two security officers, and the prisoner climbed out of their bird. The SIS group was much smaller. The prisoner had a hood over his helmet, arms cuffed behind his back, and two security officers' pistols pushed into his back on each side. The pistols were firmly pressed under the individual life-support system of his EVA suit. Everyone on both sides wore EVA suits to protect against the extremely inhospitable surface of Ganymede.

Deputy Director Jean-Luc Devis stepped forward, taking the lead. He announced, "Deputy Director."

"Director," responded Samuel Thornton.

The two men were 20 meters apart. The Ganymede Republic had officially been granted autonomy only five years and some odd months prior after several years of internal disputes. The new country's department leaders mostly held the same responsibilities as when it was under UJS rule. The intelligence department had been born out of the UJS department and its stations in the Western districts. Enough time has passed where most of the employees now were fresh blood, but occasionally you had old friends and old rivals in parallel departments in both UJS and the Ganymede Republic intelligence agencies. Devis and Thornton had been peers years prior when they both worked for the DIA as case officers.

"We have your man."

Devis motioned to a security officer, who approached with a secure data-pad. Thornton took the pad and read it.

Thornton said, "Show me his face."

Devis gestured and one of the armed officers removed the weaved hood, revealing a bruised but conscious man. The prisoner's eyes were dilated from the darkness and stung as they instantly constricted from the light on the rifles aimed at his face. He blinked a few times to clear his vision and gawked at the bold letters that spelt D.I.A. on Thornton's patch. The Deputy Director stood just a few meters away.

The prisoner immediately recognized who was taking him into custody and what that meant.

"Satisfied?" asked Devis.

The prisoner pleaded something, but no one could hear what he was saying through his muted microphone. He was visibly distraught.

"What was that?" asked Devis as he pressed a widget on his terminal to unmute the prisoner.

"-take me. Please don't let them take me." The prisoner was nearly hyperventilating now.

"Don't you worry. We'll take good care of you, comrade," said Thornton from across the dead zone between the two groups. Devis motioned to his squad. They brought the prisoner forward by pulling his arms. He was shoved over the border line by an officer. The prisoner stumbled forward and fell on the ground. Lunar dirt covered the front of his helmet visor and stained his EVA suit.

Thornton called over to the SIS party, "We won't forget this."

Devis replied, "I know."

The blaring alarms sound. Red lights flash throughout the common areas of the interior of New London.

The automated intercom continuously repeated, "Warning: Life support in all public access areas will be terminated in 30 seconds. Those who are able should bunker immediately. This is not a drill. Warning: Life support in all public access areas will be terminated in 29 seconds. Those who are..."

Chaos erupted as people panicked and scrambled in all directions. John Moore was an older man with broad shoulders who managed the local TRAS station. Everyone knew 'Mr. Moore' due to his sunny disposition and charismatic chatty nature. He was the surrogate uncle to all the local people who took the public transport on their daily commute. He seemed to know *everyone* by name.

Moore rushed through the crowd, helping people towards safety zones. He shouted, "This way! Move people!" He guided a group into a sealed chamber. Emergency doors began closing slowly.

He shouted, "Hurry!"

A woman screamed in the distance. Moore turned to see her locked behind a closing automated door with a grotesque creature that could only be created in a nightmare. She was torn apart.

The intercom bellowed, "20 seconds. Those who are able should bunker immediately. This is..."

More saw an absolute display of power and violence by the monsters attacking the citizens of New London. There wasn't time to think about who had caused this or what these crazed *things* even were. Suddenly, a young girl that he recognized tripped nearby. She couldn't have been more than six years old. The girl stumbled face first onto the ground. Two monsters charged towards her. She gaped horrified at a man kneeling next to her. Some poor bastard in complete shock, his intestines pouring out of his gashed gut. He was scooping what he could back in with red stained hands, as if that would make any difference.

Moore yelled inaudibly as he sprinted towards the girl, in an attempt to catch the predators' attention. The emergency doors were almost closed. Before the monsters reached the girl, he grabbed her hand and booked it to the nearest door in the midst of shutting.

"-all public access areas will be terminated in 10 seconds. Those who are"

Moore yelled, "Hold on!" as he held firm on her arm and

pulled her with him at full sprint. The two creatures were gaining on them. With a final burst of speed, Mr. Moore hurled the girl through the narrowing gap. She tumbled to safety.

"Life support in all public access areas will be terminated in 5. 4. 3. 2."

The door was inches from closing. Mr. Moore dove. Claws slashed in the air. Nails carved deep into his back as something grabbed the back of Moore's shirt.

"1."

The door slammed shut behind Moore. The creature's arm was crushed midway by the closing door panels. A ghoulish hand was still clutched around his denim shirt.

The young girl ran up to Moore and hugged him tightly.

"Thank you, Mr. Moore!"

All he could muster to do through the adrenaline and shock is lift up his hand into a thumbs up. He muttered between panting, "Don't... Don't mention it."

The life support for all public access and shared areas was deactivated. All oxygen was slowly depleted through the city filtration system without replenishment. Nothing was left alive. Only those who had made it to a private residency chamber survived. After a few more hours, the surviving creatures who had escaped into individual private residences were gunned down by security forces. Then the clean-up crew began to identify remains to carry out the dead to be recycled.

21

THE ROOM WAS HOT, HUMID, AND CONTAINED. SWEAT DRIPPED down Yuri Volkov's face in the unlisted DIA black site. The salty sweat stung his eyes and woke him up in a poorly lit room with a bag over his head and his hands tied behind his back.

"Where's Krasnyy, Yuri? We know you two are responsible for the recent attacks." The interrogator asked without preamble.

Volkov felt the pull of gravity without feeling the steady rumble of engines. So he knew he was on a moon, at least. The heat was unbearable as what felt like every pore in his body gaped open to release more and more sweat with each passing minute.

He asked again, "Where's Krasnyy, Yuri?"

Volkov stared into the direction of the voice. He could not see the interrogator through the material.

"I see. Well, allow me to introduce you to your host this

evening." Tristan Smith's voice was smooth and deep. He never told his *clients* his name. "You know, the use of enhanced interrogation techniques have been highly controversial and subject to legal *and* frankly ethical scrutiny. Albeit, at times critics do have some very convincing points. At face value, it is often refuted as an *ineffective* way to gather reliable intelligence." The interrogator sat across from Yuri Volkov. He ripped the hood off the Belter's head to reveal a weathered face with thick dark eyebrows. The bright lights caused Volkov to squint.

"The way I see it: if it weren't *marginally* effective, it wouldn't be in practice for tens of thousands of years. Hell, I'd even be out of a job. All intel recovered is subject to scrutinous cross-examination, and even then, even for information received through non-violent or more, how do you say, coercive methods, it is only reliable a fraction of the time. With more time, perhaps, a more *diplomatic* arrangement could be agreed upon." With two successful attacks and one failed one within the past month, time was the one thing the United Jovian System was short on.

"In more *barbaric* times, interrogators would simply remove a hand to show they meant business." He pulled out his 18 cm Martian Steel combat knife and rubbed his finger down the blade softly as he continued. "Thankfully, we are no longer barbarians. We are *civilized*," He gave a toothy grin and pointed the tip of the blade towards Yuri as he spoke, "I am *convinced* that through proper communication and teamwork we can come to a mutually beneficial agreement."

"Piss off."

"Have we not been hospitable? If not, please do let me know. It is important for me to learn about your experience so I can better cater to your needs and expectations." Volkov remained silent and maintained eye contact. The Belter had a subconjunctival hemorrhage in his left eye. A bright red smear temporarily stained the white of his eyeball.

Smith sighed. He casually dropped the blade onto a tray and the loud clank reverberated off the walls. The interrogator pulled his chair closer to Yuri Volkov, who had his arms tied behind his own chair. Smith pulled Volkov's legs apart, with a firm grip on top of his thigh where the bullet hole had entered. He gripped tighter. Volkov winced.

"I was informed you've been given state-of-the-art medical treatment. Say what you will about the UJS, and I know historically *you*, my friend, you have had a lot to say, but inhospitality is not our reputation."

Volkov sniffed then spat in Smith's face. He laughed and wiped his face with a handkerchief, before striking Volkov in the face with the back of his hand. Distant muffled screams were heard through the wall.

"Do you hear that?"

"Fuck off."

"That's your friend. You see, your little friends in the SIS gave him to us." That caught his attention.

"Bullshit."

Smith smiled. "Alright, friend. Believe what you want." He leaned back in the chair facing Volkov, their knees were still touching. "Luke Cooper. No fingerprints, no record, clean slate. Must have some friends in high places."

"Cheap tricks do not scare me. What happens next, there is no contingency plan for. The attacks will continue to get worse until Ganymede is free from autocrats like you. The blood is on your hands," said Volkov.

More distant screams continued in the next room. Volkov kept his face directly at Smith, but his eyes glanced at the noise.

"Wondering what they're doing to your friend Coop? He wouldn't say a peep to the feds in the Ganymede Republic. Those amateurs. Once we got a hold of him, well, let's just say he's singin' like a canary."

Asher Cohen turned around to Samuel Thornton behind the two-way mirror. Volkov and Smith were on the other side. Field officers are typically not directly involved in interrogation operations. Instead, specialized personnel or contractors may be tasked with such duties. In the observation room were other Defense Intelligence Agency officials, a seasoned Navy Corpsman to provide medical care if needed, technical support staff managing the surveillance equipment, and a legal advisor for the Department of Justice. Under the UJS Constitution, non-Jovian citizens did not have rights.

"Any updates on the Luke Cooper chat? The kid's been in there for 13 hours. Hopefully he knows more than that kid in the bomber vest. Just another cog in the machine, I suppose," asked Thornton.

"Yeah." Cohen responded. "His point of contact is someone named T.J. Jones. Currently breaking down the details. Let me run a search." Cohen typed into his terminal. "I think he's-"

"In deep shit?"

"Yes, but according to his profile, Jones is a Ganymede First activist and event organizer."

"You have two choices, Yuri. Either you tell us what we want to know, or you take a little stroll in the airlock."

"I tell nothing, Jovian pig."

Smith's mirth was the same manner a parent would at their own child misunderstanding a formative lesson. "You are confused, my friend. This isn't a negotiation. It's a simple matter of cooperation. Try to see things from my perspective. We have a lot in common, actually."

"I am nothing like *you*. I will never betray my comrades."

"Is that so?"

"Da."

"Just the Ganymedeans that live East of the border?"

Volkov did not respond.

Smith asked, "Collateral damage?"

Volkov remained silent. His eyes narrowed.

The interrogator clapped his hands together one time. "Okay then. You know, I was *actually* beginning to like you. I was thinking to myself, hey, this man has *integrity*. He's a reasonable person who wants to protect his people... but I've got to be honest with you, Yuri, I really do. I'm *disappointed* by your response. If you aren't willing to talk, then I suppose you'll enjoy the view from the outside. Shall we?"

With a subtle gesture, two figures emerged from the darkness behind Volkov. Each grabbed him by an arm and dragged him in his chair back. As they moved him, the pressurized door of a smaller compartment opened. One figure double checked the security of the straps in place for the terrorist, gave a thumbs up, and both walked out of the compartment room. The interrogator typed into an external terminal and the pressurized door sealed behind him. Yuri Volkov sat unattended, with his arms tied behind his back, and his legs tied to his chair, alone in an airlock. Outside of the airlock remained the interrogator at a control panel.

The interior of the airlock's metallic walls were lined with control panels, switches, and indicators for pressure, temperature, and oxygen levels. The chamber itself was small and confined with enough room for only a few bodies. Unlike every other airlock that Volkov had been in, this one did not have an emergency release handle on the inside.

The human body simply did not evolve to survive in a near total vacuum. It gets ugly pretty quick. In a mere four seconds, the skin, eyes, and tongue succumb to the cruel effects of zero air pressure as moisture boils away. At eight seconds, internal organs begin to rupture. Unconsciousness occurs within fifteen seconds accompanied by the rupture of eardrums. At thirty seconds, blood begins to boil. Humans can endure a little over 90 seconds in near-total vacuum conditions before succumbing to death.

Back to the airlock.

"The room you're in is currently a comfy 14.7 PSI. It doesn't have to be like this, Yuri. We can stop any time you want. Just tell us where Krasnyy is."

"Fuck you!"

"I appreciate your feedback."

Smith stood on the outside of the massive sealed door. He typed into the wall terminal and pulled a small lever. This triggered depressurization. The air began to slowly drain from the internal chamber Volkov occupied. The compressor engines whirred as they worked. Volkov couldn't help but watch the PSI display slowly trickle down in numerical order. A loud pinging noise triggered at every percentage point drop. Once the number hit 10.0 PSI, Smith pulled the lever back up.

"This is the average pressurization of a transport vessel. Right now isn't too bad, is it, Yuri? I want you to be honest with me. This doesn't have to be draconian. Help me help you. You want to protect Ganymede. I want to protect Ganymede. It's a win-win here. Just tell me where Krasnyy is."

Volkov remained silent and held his chin high. This is where things got interesting. Smith pushed a separate lever down on the lever as the pressure began to rise. Volkov was relieved. Until the number started to climb past 14.7 PSI. The room started to feel slightly tighter. Smith stopped at 29.4 PSI.

Minus the bullet wound, his injured eye, and his limbs strapped to a chair, Volkov was relatively comfortable. He'd been trained for torture during his former special operation days and had endured far worse, at least so far.

After a restless recess, Smith pulled another lever. The PSI began to drip down. Volkov's eyes were transfixed on the beeping and display of each point dropping down. As the PSI dropped past 10 PSI, he became dizzy. Smith stopped decompressing at 5 PSI. Volkov's hands began to shake. Nitrogen bubbles within Volkov's muscular tissue and veins began to expand. He gasped for air.

"This can all end right now, Yuri. Part of the psychological trauma of torture lies in the anticipation of recurring pain, as those subjected to torture often dread the repetition of the agonizing experience. This anticipation can compound the psychological distress, amplifying the overall trauma you're experiencing. That's the gambit. This is what you wanted. This is it."

Smith brought the pressurization back to 14.7 PSI. Volkov took in deep breaths. His eyes were throbbing.

"Is this... all... you've... got?"

"Do you think I like doing this, Yuri? I got to be honest with you, I really do, I do like it, but do I have to? Also, yes. I guess the *real* question is, what's it going to be: truth ... or dare?"

"I...will...never...talk."

"What's that, Yuri?"

"I'm..." He coughed and continued, "ready..."

"For more? You're unbreakable! You got it."

Volkov's eyes widened as the pressure suddenly crashed down to 2 PSI. He gasped as his head bobbed forward. The room began to grow fuzzy before he was able to catch his breath as the pressurization rose back to 10 PSI.

"Nine seconds at 2 PSI and you're already falling asleep on me?" Smith's voice boomed over the comm system inside the airlock chamber.

Volkov hunched his head forward over his lap as he emptied his stomach. In the low gravity it didn't plummet straight down. Some of it splashed off himself and the puke floated mid-air and splashed onto his face and hair.

"Good grief. That's disgusting. We should do something." A horrified Cohen turned away from the two-way mirror. Some of the more reserved staff members in the observation room couldn't stand the sight of vomit. One officer promptly excused herself to spill her own guts in the latrine.

Cohen asked Thornton, "Isn't this torture?"

"Technically, it's an *enhanced interrogation technique*. The methods were sent to the Department of Justice, who agreed it was in fact *not torture*. The Attorney General *and the President* both cleared it. It's above board."

"Could an argument be made that this is, more or less, a case of a department investigating itself and finding no wrongdoing?"

"Something like that."

Cohen asked, "What can we do?"

"Nothing you can do," replied Thornton.

"Well, we can't find out anything if he's dead!"

"The current administration *prefers* to kill terrorists than to capture and interrogate. This is a special exception. Just let the man work. He knows what he's doing."

Water splashed against Volkov's face, waking him. He was still tied against the chair. The airlock door was open and back to a normal pressure. A vein in his other eye had ruptured. He now had identical subconjunctival hemorrhages in both sides of his face. Everything hurt. Smith could smell the defiled man before him. He stinketh.

The interrogator returned back to the interrogation room and sat on top of the desk facing the terrorist, kicking his feet back and forth. Smith took a sip of his hot coffee and held the mug with both hands. "We've been at this for hours, Yuri. But you and I both know how this ends."

He broke eye contact from the interrogator's penetrating gaze. Volkov's throat burned. "Alright. Alright" He coughed deep and coarse. A few blood droplets remained floating in the air. "Please ... stop. I'll tell you."

"I swear on my mutha's life, Yuri, if you're lying to me right now, this will not end well for you." He set his mug down and pointed his fingers at Volkov as he spoke. "I will find out if you're lying to me. Friends don't lie to each other. So if I find out you're lying to me, we will spend some more time with Mr.

Airlock. Okay? Tell me the truth. As *your friend*, are you being honest with me?"

Volkov slowly nodded with what little strength he had left.

"I need to hear it from you, Yuri. Are you going to tell me the truth?"

Volkov grunted a barely audible "da."

Smith performed a small fist pump and stood up. He grinned and said, "Now *that's* what I'm talkin' about! Wasn't so hard, was it? I told you, I'm a reasonable man. I got to tell you, Yuri, this is one of *the best* decisions you have ever made!"

He snapped his fingers in rapid succession at one of the guards. "Hey! Get a Corpsman in here to tend to our friend."

"The son of a bitch did it," exclaimed Cohen.

Thornton warned, "Don't celebrate just yet."

"Now, let's talk about your friends and their plans," said Smith after the terrorist had regained his composure a few days later.

Yuri Volkov finally began to share some of his secrets with a quivering voice.

22

"Have you ever had a Godfather?" Alex Turner asked as he mixed various liquors over ice into two separate glasses. Samuel Thornton's corner office was chilly due to the adjacent window walls facing planetside towards Jupiter. The red and cream colored swirls of the planet's thick atmosphere placed a faint glow over the room. Windows throughout the building employed a vibration system to counter surveillance. This tech prevented laser microphones from picking up classified conversations.

"I don't think you mean in the spiritual sense," replied Thornton. He checked his watch and was surprised it was already 2 in the morning. Where did the time go?

"No, it's a cocktail." Turner handed the glass to Thornton.

"Either way, I can't say that I have. You know, the Belter's say *za zdorov'ye* when they cheer. It means *to health.*"

"Well, za zdravie," replied Turner.

The two clinked their drinks together, tapped the bottom of the glasses on the desktop, and drank.

Thornton examined the drink. He swirled it around, sniffing it, and then tasted it again. "Is that almond?"

"Yup. Amaretto. Equal parts Mariner Valley Amaretto and Jovian Whisky served on the rocks."

Thornton sipped at his drink. "I heard that in the Belt, if you can't work, they feed you to the recyclers."

"Allegedly."

"I saw it on a news report on JNN."

"You and I are not immune to propaganda, friend."

"After the hell that's been this week, I need this. Thank you, Alex."

"How's your nephew?"

Thornton found himself in the role of legal guardian and surrogate parent to his teenage nephew after his sister, a research scientist, succumbed to cancer a few years prior. Her death was attributed to her field research where she was at higher risk to radiation due to proximity to Jupiter. Despite advancements in medical science, there are still some things technology can't fix, yet. Shielded environments like domes and underground facilities provided protection against radiation, but those engaged in fieldwork faced greater exposure. Thornton's brother-in-law, a DIA accountant, met a tragic end when GRPA terrorists bombed a TRAS station during *the Troubles*. Samuel Thornton never had children of his own, but had taken his nephew in when his sister could no longer care for him, months prior to her death.

"Fine. Not doing too well in calculus right now, despite this very expensive tutor. With everything going on, I haven't been able to spend a lot of time with him. After this shit is over, I'm going to make up for lost time. Maybe take him to a Cyclones game."

"They've had a hell of a season this year. Cohen did fill me in a bit, but you know, it's need-"

"To know. Yeah yeah. I think you're cleared for this. If not, I am clearing you for it right now." Thornton took a sip of the drink and ended up finishing the remaining amount in one gulp. "God damn that's good." This brought a chuckle from Turner.

"Do you want another?"

"I shouldn't."

"No one lives forever."

Turner made him another drink. Thornton took the glass from Turner and said, "Ah, what the hell? Why not?"

"What's been going on, Sam?"

"Alright. He hasn't told us much or he doesn't know much, which, I'm not super convinced of. He has told us there is a mole. He found out about it in a roundabout sort of way."

Turner sat across from Thornton in another chair and leaned forward with full attention.

"How did that happen?"

Thornton continued, "We had a field agent working Ganymede First. Their mole in our department found out, and ratted them out to their friends. Op' went dark, we don't know if she's dead or alive. Complete radio silence. Yuri Volkov is one tough motherfucker, either he genuinely doesn't know much, which I find hard to believe, or he has the most extreme endurance I've ever seen."

"Could it be that he has only been told enough information as needed?"

"Possibly." Thornton finished off the second cocktail. "I think I need to slow down. I've gotten a headache already." Thornton stood up and stumbled slightly. He found his balance as he placed his hands and leaned onto his desk.

"Woah, easy there, lightweight. You seem a little flushed."

"Just a little dizzy, that's all. I think I need to slow down and drink some coffee."

Turner pulled out a bottle of water from the mini fridge beneath Thornton's desk and handed it to the Deputy Director. He asked, "Do you know who found out about DEADTOOTH?"

This commanded Thornton's attention the same way a bomb would.

"DEADTOOTH?"

"The Jovian mole infiltrating Ganymede First."

"I never told you what the operation name was. . ."

Thornton dropped the opened bottle of water and clutched at his throat. The bottle bounced off the desk and spilt onto the carpet. "Call.... Help..." He called out in between gasps.

Turner stood still, simply watching Thornton squirm.

"It's a funny thing. You know, you really can't trust anyone these days. The only people that *can be* informants are those who you trust the most. Ironic. Otherwise, they wouldn't know anything that was truly valuable."

Thornton slumped down to the carpet with his back against the desk. His eyes were bulging. He had ripped his tie and shirt open in an attempt to breathe better. Thornton began to drool down his chin from excessive salivation.

"I wasn't sure if whisky would pair well with cyanide. Apparently it has a flavor similar to almond, but only an absolute madman would test that out. C'est la vie. Bottoms up!"

Turner finished his drink and set the empty glass on the desk next to Thornton's. He pulled his jacket off the back of his chair and put it on one arm at a time. He straightened his cuffs and tie in a mirror. Turner walked back to the desk and locked eye contact with his boss. "Do svidaniya, old friend."

Turner watched as Thornton gasped his final breath.

23

TWO GUNSHOTS FIRED IN THE NEXT ROOM. A STARTLED, WIDE-eyed nurse screamed and ran out the treatment room. As she left, the nurse yelled, "I *do not* get paid enough for this shit."

The commotion woke up Yuri Volkov, who was laying down with a slight incline in an enclosed chamber. All things considered, he was relatively comfortable. He felt like shit, his body was beat to shit, but he had proper medical treatment and strong medicine to compensate for his experience. To recover from decompression sickness, a patient typically is placed in a hyperbaric chamber that increases the pressure around the person to force excess nitrogen out of the body and reduces the size of gas bubbles that have formed in tissues and blood vessels. Volkov's hyperbaric chamber was pressurized with 100% oxygen to help to improve oxygenation of tissues and speed up the elimination of nitrogen. He had been in the chamber for several hours as pressure was gradually reduced back to normal.

Blood seeped through under the door and pooled together. After a few moments, the handle slowly turned. The door creaked as it slowly opened. Volkov had an obstructed view in the chamber. Two figures walked through the door, a sharp dressed man holding a duffel bag in one hand and holding a medical assistant by her arm in the other. He shoved her forward towards the decompression chamber.

Through the glass, he heard a muffled command. "Open it. Now."

"It may be too early. He could get-"

The frantic medical assistant was interrupted by a standard issue Laika RD-2 pistol dug into her cheek bone. The metal felt cold against her squished face.

"Open it."

The medical assistant wept as she shakily adjusted valves to allow the controlled release of compressed air in the pressurized chamber. Before a patient could be released, they had to be ventilated. The hyperbaric chamber hissed as it released air. She worked the specialized seals that maintained pressure. The medical assistant turned a few handles and released the lock. The door slid open. Volkov turned his attention to the assistant.

The man with the gun directed, "Get out of here."

The medical assistant was in shock and too scared to move.

"Hey bitch. Leave. Now."

She came to, realized what was going on, and ran out of the door. She tripped on the pool of blood and stumbled a few feet, but caught her balance, and continued running through the brightly lit halls. Red footprints followed her path until they faded away.

The man with the gun walked up to the chamber and ripped out the IV drip out of Volkov's arm with a quick yank.

"Did you come to finish the job?"

"Not quite."

"Who are you?" asked Volkov.

"Ivan. I'm here undercover. Krasnyy is extracting us."

The two locked forearms in a handshake. Ivan, also known as Alex Turner, pulled Volkov to his feet. He stood but was disoriented by the generous dose of pain medicine.

Ivan continued, "We don't have much time. Let's go."

"About god damned time."

The two scurried through the hall, stepping over two dead Marines, and continued through the facility. Volkov was only wearing a medical gown, which was flapping as he ran. His bare ass exposed. It was quite chilly.

As they ran, Volkov drifted behind Ivan. They turned another corner and Ivan instructed Volkov to wait unseen. Ivan holstered his gun before casually walking up to two soldiers in front of the airlock.

"Alex! Do you know what is going on?"

Ivan greeted the two with firm handshakes. "Shit, I don't know. Do we have any spare EVA? I want to get out of here before we go under lockdown."

"Yeah, sure, man." One of the soldiers turned to open the locker. Ivan turned to the soldier standing next to him, grabbed the soldier's own strapped gun and pointed it up to the soldier's chin. Ivan pulled the trigger. He turned the gun, still strapped around the deceased, and blasted the other soldier in the back of the head within a split second. The ole 1-2.

Volkov ran out from behind the corner. He bent over gasping for breath. As a young buck, he had been carved from stone and been quite the heartbreaker. Power and time had made him (and his waistline) complacent in his golden years.

Ivan asked, "Are you good?"

Volkov stared at Ivan dead center with his dual subconjunctival hemorrhaged eyes. Deep red filled up almost the entirety of the whiteness around his irises. He said with the thickest accent, "I am not dead, *yet*."

Ivan pointed his finger at Volkov and cheered.

He grabbed a tactical combat EVA suit from the recently unlocked locker and opened his duffel bag. He pulled out two harnesses and an additional rig with two adjustable leg straps and two D-ring attachment straps. He tossed one at Volkov and the two began suiting up. Ivan checked both of their equipment and attached the two harnesses together with a locking strap. The men walked into the airlock. Ivan initiated manual override and started the atmospheric cycling sequence. After the room had decompressed, Ivan activated the industrial door to open to an exposed Ganymede crust.

Only a few major settlements were in domes across the

Galilean Moons and dozens of smaller moons orbiting Jupiter. Majority of the settlements were subterranean to protect against radiation and space debris. Some buildings, like this one, had an exposed airlock to dock. The facility had been built into the side of a fjord wall. The airlock was in a docking station that crudely projected from the side of the cliff wall. A deep crevice dangled beneath. This allowed for airborne vehicles to pull up next to this facility to dock and undock without many obstacles.

Ivan turned to Volkov and grabbed the front of his EVA suit with both hands. He kicked off the airlock. Ivan pulled Volkov with him. As the two free-fell for a few seconds, Ivan pulled a strap on his rig. A balloon with a flashing beacon launched into the air above them. A Tereshkova RD-21 Hellion, a multi-mission, tiltrotor military aircraft, flew overhead to the balloon beacon.

The RD-21 was also known as a "Goose" due to its bulbous shape resembling the Terran bird. Tiltrotor technology allowed it to take off and land vertically like a helicopter and transition to forward flight like a fixed-wing aircraft by tilting its rotors. This design was ideal for extracting operators from a low atmospheric environment, like a Galilean moon, and taking them to an intrastellar vessel in high orbit.

The Goose's rear compartment module hooked the balloon beacon and began withdrawing the rope as it continued to fly away from the facility. When the rope had pulled the two attached men aft of the aircraft, the loading bay doors opened.

Two people safety-tethered in EVA suits stepped out on the ledge. They each grabbed a man and pulled them onto the bay door, and immediately hooked their harnesses to a safety tether. All four people climbed inside the ship as the loading bay door closed and the Goose flew off into the sunset.

24

A HANDFUL OF HEAVILY ARMORED COMMANDOS WERE STRAPPED in the back of the ship headed to Europa. The faint hum of the accelerating engine vibrated through their seats.

It has long been suspected that alien life may exist on Europa, at least in a primitive prokaryotic form. A few hundred years ago, a second-wave of explorers discovered microbial life on Europa. Albeit, it turned out to be stow-away bacteria from Earth that came with the original explorers years before. The alien life they're hoping for will have evolved independently from Earth's influence. Due to this potential breakpoint, Europa is a territorial reserve, off limits for corporate or residential expansion. It does host a research center that is a permanent home to a small population of a thousand people.

After consulting with the Secretary of Defense, Director of Intelligence Danielle Freeman sent Asher Cohen, six Marines Spectres, and in consolidation with the Ganymede Republic,

Elsie Harper to an undisclosed location on Europa. This motley crew made up the consolidated Team Sierra. With such short notice, this was all that was approved by the pencil pushers with little in-field experience and many vocal opinions. The plan was simple: send in a small team to identify and extract Yuri Volkov.

SecDef had warned against putting Harper into this joint operation, but was overridden to show good faith and unity between the two nations. In retrospect, throwing her into the fray may not have been the best idea.

Volkov claimed ignorance to the whereabouts of Krasnyy, but interrogator Tristan Smith had a rather brilliant idea. Volkov was in need of some dental work. It was proposed to place a tracking device into a crown that would be installed on Volkov's tooth. Something like this would be too bold and they went back to the drawing board. The tracking device was instead embedded within the threading material used to stitch the wound on Volkov's leg. When Volkov escaped, they simply followed the tracking device to the current location. They did not know Thornton or the Marines on-site were going to be murdered, but they did know a mole was in the facility and would likely help Volkov escape. Sometimes you have to lose the battle to win the war.

Team Sierra arrived at Europa decelerating from a sustained 2G burn on a Tereshkova A240 Colossus, a six-engined military air transport spaceship. Each person wore an Aspis Mark II EVA Suit, with the UJS patch of Jupiter on the left shoulder, and were equipped with Laika KH-13 6.5 mm semi-automatic rifles as their primary weapon. As Europa grew larger from a small marble to the enormous rock they were about to land on, Harper was enamored with its beautiful tiger stripes.

Due to minor fluctuations or disturbances in the spacecraft's trajectory due to variations in Europa's atmospheric density or other factors, the flight crew was enduring heavy turbulence. At least heavy for non-terrestrials who grew up on rocks with thin atmospheres and low gravity. It's all relative to personal experience.

As the ship lurched in the turbulence, the pilot said, "Raptor Three-Seven to all net: entering heavy chop. Secure all loose gear. Remain seated and strap in! Duration unknown. Standby for updates."

The cockpit was in a separate compartment module with its own atmospheric pressurization and sealed from the 'cargo.' The starcraft flew predominantly with an auto-pilot bot program, but landing on a surface was always performed by a human. Machines could dock and follow a course, even veer to avoid obstacles, but they couldn't account for every variation that came with landing on a moon or planet.

As the ship slowed down 240 kilometers West of Gan De Station, the pilot announced, "Raptor Three-Seven to jumpers: DZ inbound. Four Zero Zero meters. Green light in Three Zero seconds. Stand by."

Jupiter hung in the Northwest covering half of the horizon like an angry omen. The team aboard the boat shook off the cobwebs and did last minute checks on each other's equipment. They put on their helmets to their combat EVAs and secured a tight seal. Cohen and Harper were in the same combat uniform as everyone else. Their rifles remained in safety for the time being.

"Sierra Six to all *meat bags*: standby for green light. Oscar Meyer in two Mikes. On my mark, pop doors, execute fast rope. Acknowledge. Over," commanded Kyle Woods. The crew stood in line by the door as it slid open.

"Next time I see this *rock monkey*, I'm going to put him down for good," one Spectre said.

"Martinez, keep the line secure." Sierra Six called, "Charlie Mike. Charlie Mike. SITREP follows. Objective: insert vicinity grid Tango Whiskey 853942. Target confirmed in compound. Expect heavy resistance. Do you read me?"

"We read you, sir!" the five other Spectres screamed in concert. Harper and Cohen did not and, honestly, felt a little left out by not knowing the call and response. The ship bumped a little as it slowed down above the landing zone.

Raptor Seven-Three yelled over the intercom, "Belts!"

The Marines called back "Belts!" as they unclipped their seatbelts.

The commander directed over the main line, "Sierra Six to all callsigns: execute drop! I say again, execute drop! Let's go!" The commandos began jumping out of the ship. He continued, "Go! Go! Go! Go! Go!"

"Lock'n Load, baby!" cried Cohen.

"Ooorah!" said Harper as they bumped their rifle stocks together. The team leader pushed them both out of the aircraft. Team Sierra slid down ropes from the craft about ten meters down to the icy rock surface. The rest of the team jumped out of the ship. The transport took off immediately.

The team bolted up an incline of the rocky terrain. They jumped across a narrow crevice 10 meters across. In the light gravity, a great leap was an easy effort. Team Sierra turned around a bend to see a high-rise tower and docking station erected out of the icy terrain. A low fog covered the valley between the ledge they were running through and the tower. They continued upwards from the curve to see a plated chain link fence blocking the path on the mountain side.

"Sierra Six to all callsigns: tally objective. Bearing One-Eight-Zero, one klick. Keep your buttholes tight," he announced over the comm.

A simple line map of the terrain displayed with a flashing dot on their HUD on the inside of their helmet visors. The flash was the tracking stitches attached to Yuri Volkov. It may or may not still be in his leg. This could very well be a trap.

A Marine shot the exterior light shining on the path and another made quick work of the fence using a portable laser cutter. He cut out a man-sized hole and each person marched through.

On the other side of the fence were well lit habitat modules connected to one another. They strategically used this wide wedge in the mountainside to protect themselves from the elements. There was no one present outside the habitat modules this early in the morning. After cycling the airlock, they entered.

They walked through the hab and passed through an overgrown greenery room. The plants were breaking through glass and had crawled amongst the ground and sides of the walls.

"Right side clear!"

"Left side clear!" they announced in consecutive order as they checked each room. This first hab had no one else in it. They might have left or it was an impending ambush. The Marines exited the hab modules and kept moving.

"Target sighted. One Zero Zero meters North. Maintain concealment. Radio discipline in effect. Over," commanded the Six.

"Roge," responded another Marine.

Just ahead of the connected module's airlock exit, a few figures patrolled on a far off ledge. Between them and the ledge was a narrow man-made bridge leading to a wall and gate. The bridge was only suspended 20 meters into the air. The team was careful to remain out of sight. They crept beneath the bridge, where the lights did not reach them to the other side.

Knelt just behind a cylindrical storage container, Martinez fired his 6.5 mm rifle directly between the eyes of a guardsman. Red painted the inside of the combatant's helmet and sprayed into the air. The man crumbled to the ground and smashed his helmet face first onto the rocky terrain. As the visor cracked even further, steam of the internal suit environment sizzled into the thin atmosphere. At the same time in successive fashion, the other guardsmen dropped.

"Sierra Six, this is Two-One. Tango down, three times. Over," announced Martinez on the comm line.

The individual fire teams of the operation had their own call names to signify if they were a part of Fireteam One, Two, or Three.

High above the building walls were oscillating flood lights. The Marines tossed and kicked the bodies down into the ditch, beneath the light's shine. The limp bodies tumbled like rag dolls.

"Roger that, Two-One. Good work. Out," said Sierra Six.

Jackson swept the area in front of the building. He signaled, "Sierra Six, this is Two-Three. Area clear. Ready to advance. Over."

"All stations, this is Sierra Six. Proceed to next waypoint. Acknowledge. Over," commanded Sierra Six.

"Sierra Six, One-One. Wilco," agreed Harper from the tail end of the group.

One of the Marines typed into the terminal at the gate to trigger the unlocking mechanism. The massive gate doors wheezed and churned as they opened into the next enclosure.

As the gate slid open, the team marched through. On the other side were more modules. These weren't living quarters like before. These were larger and more rectangular shaped: laboratory modules. Two guards patrolled outside with the security lights oscillating to and fro. Sierra Six signaled for two Marines to enter into the module on the far side, two to enter the module on the left side, and for the last SOG member, Harper, and Cohen to stay with him. As the teams split up, they avoided the light and silently took out the guards as opportunity struck.

Sierra Six, Cohen, Harper, and the last Marine ran up the stairs into a facility module, cycled the airlock, and ran inside. The first room they crept in had two armed soldiers waiting for them. The two enemy combatants filled the Marine with lead. Sierra Six cursed, as they instantly turned around behind the door ledge.

Harper yelled "Frag out!" on the team's private comm line and pulled the pin out of a grenade. She underhand tossed it at an adjacent wall. The bounce from the grenade allowed it to roll behind the table the two soldiers were hiding behind. The grenade exploded and violently scattered shrapnel in all directions. The two immediate threats had been neutralized.

Sierra Six, Cohen, and Harper moved forward into the next room. As soon as Sierra Six saw another soldier, he signaled for Cohen and Harper to hold back. Sierra Six waited behind an open door. In the room he was hiding were various computers, terminals, and chairs lined up against the walls. As the light of the soldier's rifle showed through the door, Sierra Six slung his rifle back and pulled out his knife. The soldier stepped through the door into the room. From behind the door lurched Sierra Six. He slid in front of the soldier, pushing his gun and head to stage-right, and plunged his high carbon steel knife directly into the side of his now exposed neck, slicing through the EVA suit's thick material. The body dropped to the ground. He pulled out his knife, cleaned it on the corpse's clothes, and signaled for Cohen and Harper to follow.

"Target Two Five meters ahead," updated Sierra Six on the team channel.

The following room was empty. At the far end of the room two doors slide open to two large Rottweilers in body armor around their torso and neck. As they snarled and gnashed, they could see their natural teeth had been replaced with titanium alloy teeth.

"Is that... are those *dogs*?" asked Harper.

"Fuck."

"I've never seen one in person."

"No sudden movements," said Sierra Six with his hand held out. The three of them slowly spread apart in the room as the two Rottweilers walked towards them, snarling.

Sierra Six checked his left and saw a separate door, the dogs now separated Cohen and Harper from himself. "I'm going to lock them in that storage closet. Regroup at the RV. I'll find you."

One Rottweiler was pacing towards Harper when it stopped in its tracks. The two dogs turned and bolted at the Six who banged the cabinets to draw their attention. He ran around the corner and blurs of black and brown terror followed at full speed. Their gallops gained even more distance in the light gravity. Kyle Woods could not think of anything more terrifying than an aggressive animal in this setting. Not only were they entirely unfamiliar with how dogs acted in real life due to lack of exposure, and education on such matters was not important this far from Earth, but there's also the cognitive difference between killing an enemy with a gun vs an animal who doesn't know any better. It's not as if horses who valiantly rode into battle in cavalries were complacent or consenting to the wars they were helping in.

Cohen and Harper bolted through to the next room.

"Break. Break. Break." It was Martinez's voice crackling over the radio.

"Lima Charlie. Cohen, send it."

"SITREP. Over."

Cohen said over the team comm line, "Two-man element still in the fight. Harper and Cohen." His radio talk was a bit rusty from no longer being active duty. He should have used their call signs of One-One and One-Two.

Martinez responded, "Two Tangos down but ambulatory. Three-One and Three-Two got their wings clipped, but they're mobile and moving to extract. Two-Three and I are still in contact. What's your status? Over."

In between ferocious muffled barks in the background, Sierra Six updated his team. "Got the pups locked up and secure. We're Oscar Mike to the RV."

Cohen and Harper crept through the facility trying to regroup. The next room they found was a long empty hall with tall glass chambers on parallel sides. The chambers were filled with liquid and floating bodies of deformed human beings of all ages and sizes.

"What is this?" asked Cohen.

"I think this is where they grow the reapers."

"Do you think they *grow* them?"

"I'm not sure."

Martinez called over the radio signal, "Pretty sure they're bioengineered, not grown fresh. Just a guess."

Sierra Six called out on the radio signal, "Martinez, on your left."

Martinez responded on the radio, "One-One. One-Two."

No response.

Martinez cleared his throat and yelled their actual names since they didn't respond to their call signs, "Cohen. Harper. Where are you two?"

"We're in some sort of laboratory."

"This place is disgusting," commented Cohen.

"Does anyone have visual on target anymore?" asked Martinez.

"No, but he's in here. The last signal from him was 15 minutes ago. He might be hiding in a panic room that blocks the signal, or an equivalent," responded Sierra Six.

"All stations, this is Two-One. Continue advance to grid Echo-Four-Seven. Rally point marked on ATAK," Martinez said. A rally point appeared on the map of the building inside all of their helmet visors.

Harper and Cohen kept walking towards the end of the chambered room they were in. He checked his interior map which indicated that the rendezvous point was just ahead. On the opposing wall were two tall doors sealed together. Without a terminal or button, the two investigated the wall to see if there was any way to access the room. A small camera in the room rotated to watch them.

Harper set her utility pouch down and pulled out a small metal box. After flipping a switch and extending the limbs of the box, it resembled a large spider. She pressed the device onto the center of the doors' seal. The limbs of the machine extended to attach to each separate door. From the tool's anterior side emerged a dual pronged wedge that inserted itself into the seal. It whined and gave a mechanical hiss and the machine slowly forced opened the sealed doors a meter apart.

Harper saw two armed men within view. She set her barrel through the door opening and made quick work of the two soldiers.

This gave Cohen and Harper enough space to duck underneath the device and walk into the next room. They stopped just short of the two freshly made corpses. A voice from beyond the wall called out to them. They would think about the next few minutes every day for the rest of their lives.

Martinez and Jackson moved through dimly lit corridors. Martinez walked to a hallway corner and froze.

"Enemy contact!"

A roar echoed through the hall and Jackson booked it to the edge of the corner wall and peered around with his rifle held high, eyes set to kill.

A massive reaper charged at Martinez. Jackson pulled his trigger and fired a three-round burst. The reaper dropped to the ground dismembered. They swept the room but didn't see any more threats.

Martinez approached the remains to inspect it.

"What the hell is it?" asked Jackson.

Martinez kicked the reaper. It didn't move.

"This one's different than those small fuckers back on Gany. Looks like some kind of mutated *bear*."

"Nah, for sure some kind of animal. Cross bred, genetically modified, or something."

"Looks like some performance mods." He kicked the body over to lay on its back as he lifted an arm with the barrel of his rifle to inspect. "Definitely a bear."

"I thought they were way bigger than that? A small bear, maybe. More like a wolverine."

"I don't think wolverines are that big."

"Incoming."

"Trust me."

Jackson had enough. "Martinez, radio discipline. What was that?"

"Incoming!" Sierra Six yelled over the comm system. They heard another roar from the next room. Sierra Six burst through the doors of the hall Martinez and Jackson were in as a second reaper bear/wolverine charged behind him.

Sierra Six yelled, "Move!"

The trio sprinted down the corridor, the reaper in hot pursuit. After a few sudden turns, they ran into an interior laboratory. The automated doors slid shut. Martinez shot the door user interface, sealing the sliding doors in place. The reaper continuously smashed against the door.

The three noticed Alex Turner/Ivan standing across the room, holding a terrified civilian in a lab coat at gunpoint. The SOG team had no idea who either of them were.

Ivan said, "One more step and she dies!"

Martinez, Jackson, and Sierra Six both held up their weapons at Ivan and his capture.

"Put the civvy down. Now."

Spectres don't care about hostages. That's not their mission objective. The President had previously signed an executive order that forbade intelligence agencies from killing non combatants on covert operations. Ivan incorrectly assumed that the executive order applied to all military personnel, as well. The executive order did not apply to the military.

The encrypted SATCOM crackled to life. A calm and authoritative voice filled their earpieces. "Sierra Six, this is Overlord. Target designated hostile. You are cleared hot. Repeat. You are cleared hot."

The pounding started again, but from a different door. There were three doors. One behind Ivan and his company for the evening, one sealed behind the Marines, and another adjacent to them in the lab.

He replied in a monotone voice, devoid of emotion. "Overlord, Sierra Six. Solid copy. Proceeding with extreme prejudice."

The commander tightened his grip as he delicately tried to

aim for Ivan and not the hostage. In an effort to at least *attempt* to do as little harm as possible to them.

"Affirmative, Sierra Six. Execute at your discretion."

It's wild how in times of high stress or trauma how long time can feel. Seconds can feel like days. Hours can feel like weeks.

Sierra Six put Ivan's body mass within his iron cross-hairs. The hostage whimpered with Ivan's forearm wrapped around her torso to grip her throat. He held her tight to his body.

The pounding on the door stopped. An even larger reaper bursted through the doors behind Ivan and the hostage as the three Marines pulled their triggers. In a blur of violence, the bear mauled Ivan and the civilian. The bullets bursted into its back. Blood sprayed across pristine lab equipment.

"Holy fuck!" yelled Martinez.

The bear turned with Ivan dangling from its jaws by his leg.

"Exit strategy. Now!" screamed Jackson.

The Marines bolted for another door, leaving behind the carnage. The reaper continued to feed. In the final few seconds of his life, Ivan, while hanging upside down, pulled the pin out of a grenade strapped to his armored vest. He took the reaper and hostage with him on his way out.

Cohen and Harper kept the crosshairs of their rifles on the man speaking.

"Let's be rational. We're just talking."

In the next room there was a tipped over desk with a computer terminal and monitor bashed upon the ground. Behind the desk was Yuri Volkov with a single-barrel shotgun aimed at Cohen and Harper. Near the bar was another man fixing a cocktail. Towering behind the desk was a large painting of *Saturn Devouring His Son* by the Terran artist Francisco Goya. The image was quite unsettling of the titan Saturn holding a decapitated body while eating its limbs.

"Anton Krasnyy, the *infamous* Lion of Ganymede."

"Ah, my reputation precedes me," he said as he lifted the cocktail glass to his mouth. Before he could take a sip the glass shattered as a bullet blasted through it and against the wall behind him. Krasnyy loured. "That's just poor manners. I was really looking forward to that."

Volkov didn't return fire. He was still waiting.

"Woah woah woah. Let's settle down," cried out Cohen.

Harper still had her rifle firmly pressed into her shoulder. The chamber still smoked from the shot fired.

Cohen thought the gray hair made Krasnyy appear older than he was. Krasnyy, as if reading his mind, said, "*And* you're shorter than I expected. What can I do for you, Officer Cohen?"

"You know who I am?"

"Of course. You're the feds. Here to take me away into custody to stand a *fair trial amongst my peers* for the perceived wrongdoings against *God and Country*. Quite the duo you two make. I thought that it was a nice touch that you were the man of honor at her wedding. It's a shame, Mr. Cohen. When I learned how your wife died, I can only imagine what you felt. My condolences."

Cohen didn't reply.

"And who could forget *Doctor* Elsie Harper. What a beautiful family you have."

"You really did your homework," said Harper.

"Easy, Elsie," cautioned Cohen. He had a thick skin and knew better than to let cheap words break his bones.

Harper tightened her grip on the trigger. Her aim was steadily on the man by the bar. The other rifleman had a laser sight fixed between her eyes.

Krasnyy continued, "The fight for independence isn't just against our rulers from the UJS; it's standing up against all kinds of control. As someone who formerly served the Belt, I'm standing with the people of Ganymede, not just as friends, but as family, fighting for the same cause. We've felt what it's like to be pushed around and ruled by force. But if we join together, we can shake up the powers that be and make a new era where we're free. Even though you Jovians think you're stronger, you don't know how determined we are in the West, and how strong a free Ganymede can be. And you, Dr. Harper, should be ashamed of yourself to work with our oppressors against the people you swore an oath to protect. The UJS is committing genocide."

"No. Genocide is what Ganymede First *wants* but didn't have the means to. Until you," said Cohen.

"What you're doing is not protecting people," added Harper.

"Spoil the rod and spare the child, Doctor. You of all people should know that." He took a step closer, his hands still held up by his chest. Volkov kept a steady aim at Harper. Cohen remained between Harper and the desk, with a hand out in an attempt to ease the situation.

"This is insane. How did we let this happen?" asked Cohen.

"We just wanted to be left alone while you wanted to win."

"You're sick," blurted out Harper. Cohen could see she was getting overwhelmed.

Volkov spoke up from behind the desk. "No, it is Ganymede who is sick. A united Ganymede, free from tyrant rule, is the future. We are trying to save this dead world."

"And you plan to do that by revenge?"

"No. Not revenge. *Retribution*."

"What're you planning to do then?"

"It's simple, really," explained Krasnyy. "We keep releasing WILLOW onto the public until Olympus is free."

Volkov interrupted, "I already told you this while you were torturing me like an animal."

"Bullshit. My people would *never* torture," said Harper, in denial. Torturing for information was internationally criticized as ineffective and illegal in most jurisdictions. Technically, Harper was correct as it was the UJS, not the Ganymede Republic, who had tortured Volkov.

"Your *people* did the dirty work for you." This wasn't necessarily true due to them working for separate agencies, but those are semantics that Volkov hadn't bothered to sort out ahead of time.

Cohen calmly stated, "No one else has to get hurt. Yuri Volkov and Anton Krasnyy. You're being detained for-"

Woods, Jackson, and Martinez trudged through the facility.

"I read four heart beats. Repeat, four heart beats. Two tangos. Two friendlies in the next room," said Sierra Six.

"The spooks?" asked Martinez.

Jackson responded, "Yes.".

"Ten Four. You're clear to engage the target. Happy hunting, Six," said Operations Command. Command was in high orbit around Europa. Radio delay was minimal, within microseconds.

"Thank you, Support. Over and out."

Sierra Six signaled on the radio to Cohen and Harper, "Be advised, we are in your last known position. Multiple KIA confirmed. Visual on target through Northeast door. Proceeding now!"

"Wait wait wait," said Cohen.

Martinez, Jackson, and Sierra Six burst through the door, guns blazing. Yuri Volkov pulled his trigger. The bullet struck Elsie Harper's helmet. The shattered pieces floated in the low gravity as her body hit the floor.

Martinez shot Volkov, still kneeling behind the desk, in the head, just below his eye in his left cheekbone. Krasnyy's legs were blown to shreds by Sierra Six's rifle. He collapsed to the ground as he and Martinez ran to his body, kicking away any potential weapons. Jackson kept the infrared laser attached on the barrel of his Laika KH-13 rifle aimed directly into Krasnyy's eyes, causing the terrorist temporary blindness to ensure a cooperative captive. Martinez grabbed handcuffs and clipped his arms behind his back.

"Sedate and bag him," directed Sierra Six. He addressed Command, "Sierra Six to Overlord. HVT secured. Prepare for exfil."

While Sierra Six and Martinez dealt with Krasnyy, Asher Cohen was rocking Elsie Harper back and forth in his arms. He removed her helmet. Her face and hair were soaked from the bullet wound.

He closed her fixed eyes.

There was a fine line between an intelligence agency's authority to arrest vs. detain, but the legality of it was for the lawyers to decide later. The point being: Krasnyy was coming with them one way or another. The following hours were simple and routine. The remaining soldiers in the compound surrendered upon the detainment of Krasnyy. There were not any reapers left in the facility. The guard dogs were sedated and confined to their kennels. They would be rehomed to an animal reservation on Ganymede.

Cohen leaned his head back against the seat and stared out the window. He watched the stripes of Europa's landscape get smaller and smaller until the planet was nothing more than a pale pearl dangling in the sky.

They traveled not to victory, but from victory. The trip back to Ganymede was solemn and silent. The deceased bodies were crudely stacked in the cargo container. Everyone back home was celebrating this morning as a victory but there wasn't much to smile about for those who experienced it first hand.

25

THE WEIGHTS SLAMMED AS NIKOLAI YUROVICH VOLKOV PUSHED his legs to near full extension. He was careful not to lock out his knees. With one hand, he twisted each separate handle sideways to lock into place the banded leg press machine and climbed out of the saddle. Under the light gravity, banded resistance was much more effective for weight training rather than slamming old-school iron plates. A 20 kg plate on Earth would only be 3 kg in this gravity. Hardly enough to properly stress and strengthen a young man's body.

Volkov adjusted the strap to his arm-sling and winced. He spread his legs and bent over to stretch his taut muscles. Blood seeped through his shirt as one of the stitches popped open again. He stretched through the pain. It was only one stitch. It could wait.

The young man saw something glimmer on the distant

monitor and turned up the volume. It was a breaking news report from the Jovian National News. He climbed into the harness of an *Infinity Runner* and began a light warm-up jog as he watched.

Talking heads spoke in between b-roll footage of a heavyset tall man being taken into custody with his face blurred out. The news anchor sat confidently at the news desk, surrounded by various monitors displaying news graphics and footage.

She reported, "Samuel Thornton passed away in his sleep over the weekend from what is reported to be a stroke. The Deputy Director of Operations had served in the Defense Intelligence Agency for twenty years. A small memorial will be held Sunday at Bradbury Cemetery.

"Now to our top story tonight: Timothy Jones, suspected activist with the Ganymede First international terrorist organization, has been detained.

"This development follows the recent death of terrorist Yuri Volkov, who was killed in action by the United Jovian Marine Corps during a joint operation with the DIA. In a move honoring religious beliefs, Yuri Volkov's body was not recycled. However, neither the Belt Empire nor the Ganymede Republic accepted his remains for burial."

She wanted to say, he may be rotting in hell, but he certainly isn't welcome to rot on Jovian land. Her professionalism knew better than to express how she truly felt, even if public sentiment agreed with her.

The anchor continued, "His body will be launched into Jupiter's upper atmosphere to prevent any potential future conflicts or acts of terrorism at the burial site.

"In related news, wanted terrorist Anton Krasnyy has also been apprehended. The former Belter was wanted for war crimes during the Ganymede Revolution and recent attacks on Kepler City and New London. He will be held in custody pending trial before a grand jury.

"Human rights advocates are protesting the current treatment and the stripping of citizenship from all Ganymede First activists citing this would leave them without a country and without a home.

"We'll continue to monitor these developments and bring you the *latest* updates as they unfold."

Nikolai Volkov was annoyed at the broadcast.

He flipped the channel to Ali Miller, who was bright red and practically fuming at the mouth as he ranted his bombastic speculation that the attack on New London was a setup and that Krasnyy was a DIA pys-op placed to intentionally paint Ganymede First in a bad light.

He clicked the remote again and the channel changed to poorly made reality television where confrontational and problematic strangers attempted to marry one another after recently meeting. He turned up the speed on the *Infinity Runner* and carried on.

.　.　.

Family and friends gathered around the casket of Elsie Harper. They adorned rice balls, called pindas, and with flowers at her feet. Her loved ones recited Sankhya funeral chants, paying their final respects to the deceased.

The Director of Special Intelligence (SIS), Jean-Luc Devis, took the podium and began the eulogy. In the audience were various officials from Ganymede Republic, UJS, and loved ones of Harper who came to pay their respects. Harper's two daughters held strong with somewhat apathetic and insipid expressions, as if still in shock of the whirlwind of the past few days. Harper's oldest daughter bore a strikingly similar appearance to Maria Ramirez.

Devis gave a beautiful eulogy, reminding people of the sacrifice that the men and women of the intelligence agencies and armed forces make in order to protect opportunity, welfare, national security, and peace. What was all of this for? Freedom is not free. It only survives because few stood against many. Free men and women stood in the face of tyranny and those who wished to watch their world burn. He reminded everyone that these were the values that Elsie Harper risked her life for. Devis quoted from the Bhagavad Gita, the Upanishads, and the Rig Veda, connecting the scriptures to Harper's life and sacrifice. He posthumously awarded Elsie Harper an intelligence star, one of the highest honors given within the SIS. The Director of Intelligence stepped away from the podium, leaving the crowd to reflect on his words as they mourned the loss of their beloved.

The funeral service concluded. Cohen gave a wave to Harper's family, who attempted to smile back. The Director of Defense Intelligence (DIA), Danielle Freeman, approached Asher Cohen as everyone dispersed to their after-party events.

"How are you holding up?"

"As well as can be imagined."

"I know she meant a lot to you. The timing is shit, but there's something you need to see. Your next assignment just came in. Seems our friends have been busy."

She handed Cohen a tablet displaying surveillance footage of Viktor Kessler walking with two other scientists.

You've got two options: go back to driving a desk, or help avenge the attacks on Ganymede... and Harper."

Freeman knew the answer before she even asked the question.

"The flight leaves tomorrow morning at zero five hundred hours."

"Where to?"

She told him.

He watched the funeral service. Families and friends gathering, and laughing. People enjoying memories, mourning the loss, and celebrating the life of their loved one. Cohen thought about what it meant to serve in special intelligence: putting yourself in danger for shit pay and a high risk of an early grave. More often than not, those working behind the scenes are the unsung heroes who keep civilization remotely stable, yet their names would rarely, if ever, be put in history books. Their lives would be forgotten, erased behind black operations and secret services.

Intelligence agencies' covert actions had such a bad reputation in the public perspective due to all their failures being highlighted for newsreels and clicks while all their victories remained in the dark. The most effective operations are ones the public will never learn about.

26

Captain Adam Harris stood on the bridge of the *Deimos*-class guided-missile destroyer UJF *McCarthy* en route towards the Asteroid Belt. The *Deimos*-class destroyers boasted an impressive overall length of 153 to 156 meters and a displacement ranging from 7530 to 8800 metric tonnes of pure steel and military grade firepower. Military grade doesn't mean state-of-the-art, it means it's the *bare minimum* that the military will tolerate. They still go for the cheapest product that meets the minimum requirement and fits their budgets. These formidable vessels were equipped with an arsenal of over 90 missiles, surpassing many earlier guided-missile cruiser classes in both size and firepower. It carried 323 souls: 300 enlisted crew with 23 officers. United Jovian Frigate (UJF) is the traditional ship prefix for vessels in the United Jovian Navy (UJN). Destroyers and Destroyer Escorts are named after Navy and Marine Corps heroes. The UJN's operational policy has eight destroyers escort each anti-starfighter hunter-killer group. Four DEs would provide a close screen for the DD, while the other four would flank enemy starfighters detected through scouting tech.

Captain Harris stood behind the command center console. He picked up the radio terminal and said, "Comms, this is the Captain. Initiate contact with Aristarkhov Naval Base. Use the agreed-upon frequency."

"Aye aye, sir. Initiating contact now," replied the communications officer.

The Aristarkhov Naval Base is a self-sustained series of connected stations complete with a small fleet in orbit on the outer rim of the Asteroid Belt. The military installation features six large modules or buildings, providing 3900 square meters of interior space, alongside eight inert storage bunkers with a combined 6000 square feet and five additional structures. A separate service area housed 18 modules including two barracks to support the facility's operations and personnel. Often used as a refueling station, it is the final outermost Belter stronghold before the international waters between the Belt and the Jovian System.

The entire naval base operated in true Zero G. The station personnel and staff kept their hair short or tied taut, or else it flowed as if it had a mind of its own without gravity to pull it down. Aristarkhov's crew rotated in 11 month tours to and from stronger gravity rocks like Ceres to minimize muscular and skeletal atrophy, and other biological damages that can happen in long-term microgravity. Microgravity refers to being *weightless* as if floating. This is far more dangerous physiologically than the minimal gravity of the Jovian moons.

Belter Admiral Aleksandr Sokolov received a transmission in the base defense operations center. He was alerted by a filtered radio signal.

"Aristarkhov, this is Captain Harris of the UJF *McCarthy*. Be advised, we are commencing naval exercises in international waters at..." Harris then gave the coordinates for the location using the astral coordinate system.

Sokolov put the radio terminal into his shoulder, turned to his Executive Officer (XO), the second in command for the base, and muttered off-mic in Belter. "Jovians. Always pushing boundaries."

He replied into the radio, "UJF *McCarthy*, this is Admiral Sokolov. We acknowledge your notification. What is the nature and duration of these exercises? Over." He laid on an extra thick accent purposefully when speaking to Jovians.

The Jovian Captain replied, "Admiral, exercises will include anti-starfighter warfare drills and live-fire gunnery practice. Duration is 72 hours. This is a routine operation. No cause for alarm. Over." They were close enough that there was almost no noticeable delay between call and response.

"Understood, Captain. We will be observing. Aristarkhov out."

There were upsides and downsides to this method. Your side was trained using life-fire exercises in plausible scenarios and territories, but the downside was that all of your methods were likely watched by any enemy opponents in grave detail.

Sokolov put down the radio terminal and walked to his XO. His boots magnetized to the grid floors with each step to keep him grounded in the station's microgravity. "Alert the Northern Fleet. I want eyes on every move they make."

Hilda 153 twinkled in the distance as the ship soared towards the asteroid. Operation TALON was in full effect. Black space swallowed the Cosmic Transport Dock warfare ship in a sea of black.

Krasnyy had revealed the location of a high value target without much resistance. The target was on an abandoned mining outpost on Hilda 153 that was retrofitted to be a biolab. At the asteroid's furthest distance, it occasionally crossed through Jupiter's orbit.

Krasnyy's cooperation had been far more forthcoming than Volkov's. Mostly from a desire to avoid the death penalty thanks to a very *persuasive* interrogator named Tristan Smith. That conversation officially never happened, of course.

Inside the Aristarkhov Naval Base Command Center, Admiral Sokolov leaned over a holographic map, studying the movements of the UJF vessels.

Executive Officer Petrov reported, "Sir, the Jovian exercises have moved closer to our territorial waters. They're pushing the limits of international space."

Admiral Sokolov grimaced and scratched his beard while staring at the map. He did not turn to his subordinate. "How close?"

"Just outside our outer defense perimeter."

Sokolov straightened up and his eyes narrowed. He directed, "Get me a secure line to High Command."

Anatoly gestured wildly and raised his voice even louder. "You're tellin' me you've never had bratwurst with sauerkraut?" He hiccuped and continued, "What kind of Belter are you?"

The two inexperienced ensigns were at another corner of the Asteroid Belt, on a lookout station in orbit near Hilda 153. They sat in the observation deck at the coastal radar station. Old equipment beeped softly as they drank high-octane energy drinks and swapped stories to stay awake on these long watchduty shifts.

"That's disgusting."

A small blip moved slowly across the radar screen behind them as they argued.

Dmitry pulled out a flask and took another swig. He reasoned, "Oh sure, next you'll say you put hot sauce in this vodka."

"Wait, is that a thing? We should try that!" Anatoly grabbed the flask from his buddy. There was a strict rule forbidding imbibement during any official military duty. But, what the lieutenant didn't know, didn't hurt 'em.

The blip on the radar screen grew larger before it disappeared off the edge.

"You're an imbecile. That is probably why they sent *you* to this dump. I don't even know why we're here. Fuck this backwater station. Nothing happens here."

Anatoly grinned and said, "At least we have each other, comrade!" He poured more vodka from the flask into his and his watchmate's energy drink.

Dmitry groaned. He muttered to himself, "That's what I'm afraid of."

An alarm blared and the young drunk men jumped in their seats.

Anatoly slurred, "What's that?"

"Nothing. You worry too much."

Aristarkhov alerted the entire defense network that there were UJS drills happening this weekend. Dmitry pressed a button and the screeching noise stopped. "It's probably just another alarm for that. This radar is a faulty piece of shit. Remember last time there were scheduled wargames and it went off?"

"Fuck gettin' chewed out by Lieutenant. I am not waking him up again."

"I'm telling you, dude. It's nothing."

"Yeah. You're probably right."

Dmitry hiccuped and said, "Always am."

.   .   .

"Sidewinder Actual, this is TALON Lead. We are Oscar Mike to objective. ETA three hours. Over." The filtered voice boomed in the large room's sound-system.

Danielle Freeman was a fly on a wall at the back of a fully occupied command center. Various leaders and officials of MARCOM huddled over a holographic map-covered table with the rest of the twin operations' command team. Blinking screens filled the walls. TALON and APACHE were on their own due to the time delay. A radio signal took 42 minutes to travel one-way from the outer rim of the Asteroid Belt to the moons of Jupiter.

"APACHE is green across the board. SIGINT confirms Northern Fleet's at full alert, eyes locked on our fleet movements." The entire Belter Navy was focused on the wargames.

The Secretary of Defense turned to the National Security Advisor and quoted, "Abandon all hope, ye who enter."

Freeman prayed quietly in the back, "This better work."

The wargames had been ravaging on for nearly 26 hours. The crew of the station alternated in three 8-hour shifts. Sokolov and Petrov were already on their second shift for this weekend.

"Admiral Sokolov, Jovian vessels are approaching territorial waters."

"Understood, Petrov. How close?"

"Too close for comfort, sir. No indication they're planning an attack on Aristarkhov, but their proximity is concerning. Should we request for additional support?"

There is no way they would risk attacking a naval base with only one destroyer and its escorts. It would be suicide if they did. But why would they be so close? the Admiral wondered.

"Should we request additional support?"

"Negative. High Command orders to maintain current posture. Monitor and hold fire. If they get too close, lock on to send a warning. Hold targeting until my command."

The crew inside the Aristarkhov Naval Base Command Center began to sweat. The Admiral refused to start a war over what was likely a misunderstanding.

UJS didn't have time to ask for permission from the Belt, let alone on the off-chance that the permission would be even granted for the exfiltration, there was a risk that the information would leak and the high value target would be notified to escape. SecDef had instructed everyone to keep this operation tighter than a nun's asshole. Her words, not mine. They were wrong. The Belt would've turned over terrorists who were acting on their own accord, especially those guilty of crimes against humanity. The Belt may disagree on political policy, but they're not animals. They still cared about human life and justice.

The exfiltration team were under strict orders: bag 'em and grab 'em. Due to the time-delay between the Belt and Ganymede, hands-on officers acted as on-site real-time command for the mission.

Cohen pivoted in a chair behind the command console and

pressed a button on his helmet to signal to all units. "Just received confirmation from Command. Operation is green. H-hour minus eighty Mikes. Stand by to execute."

Alarms blared as sailors rushed to their stations inside the UJF *McCarthy*'s combat information center. Captain Adam Harris leaned over a tactical display.

A red light flashed. The radar operator instantly knew what it signaled. He announced, "Multiple SAM systems active. Painting our ship. Over."

"Copy that. All stations, maintain alert posture," the Captain commanded his crew.

A Communications Officer reported an incoming transmission from Aristarkhov Naval Command.

Captain Harris instructed him to patch it through.

The seasoned face of a Belter appeared on the main display. A deep voice spoke through the filtered intercom, "Captain Harris, this is Admiral Sokolov. Again. Your wargames have crossed the line. You are near violation of trespassing in Belter territorial waters."

"Admiral, This is a sanctioned exercise. You were notified-"

Sokolov interrupted, "Negative. I approved drills within provided coordinates only. Pull back immediately or we take defensive action."

Harris discretely asked his XO, "How close are we to the boundary?" The Captain left the microphone on. Their conversation could be heard faintly through the broadcast.

The Executive Officer checked a few displays and told the Captain the distance. Harris turned his attention back to Sokolov.

"Admiral, we are *within* your expanded security zone. Exercise poses no threat-"

A warning klaxon cut him off.

"Red Crown, Red Crown! Two bogey inbound, repeat, two bogey inbound. Bearing 030. Intercept course. Confirmed anti-ship cruise missiles on lock."

Harris spoke to Sokolov, "Call off your men, Admiral. Do not escalate this."

"Withdraw. You have ten minutes"

The transmission cut.

Harris directed his men, "All stations, this is Stargazer. Set condition one throughout the ship and support. CAP, intercept incoming bandits. Weapons tight. No provocative actions. I repeat, weapons tight."

The UJF *McCarthy* had the full attention of the Belter Armed Forces.

Despite TALON being a capture only operation, that only applied to the high value targets. There was killing to be done. Fortunately, they had some stroke of fortune in getting past the sentinel post undetected.

After forcing docking procedures to the former mining facility on the asteroid Hilda 153, the doors would not unseal.

Three Marines carried a meter long portable railgun to the seal.

Forced entry was necessary, as Belter encryption was beyond the current capabilities of UJS Navy Intelligence.

After securing the footing, the railgun was triggered. A loud whine pierced the pressurized air as the weapon charged. Electromagnetic force propelled tungsten projectiles through the door. The tungsten struck like lightning. After the breach, six Spectres swept silently through the smoke into the quiet corridors. Cohen was appointed liaison between Command on Ganymede, APACHE, and TALON.

"Red Six, visual on two tangos. Proceed with takedown." The enemy figures were dressed as mercenaries, not as Belter military personnel.

"Copy that, Ironbar. Engaging."

Lieutenant Commander Kyle Woods led the ground team forward. He and another Spectre pulled their triggers. Two quick fires bursted as the guards went limp. Their boots were still magnetized to the metal floors, so the bodies swayed in a lifeless dangle while staying fully erect. Woods was well seasoned, but this was the other Marine's first time killing. It was easier than he thought it would be. He imagined an internal governor would prevent him from actually pulling the trigger, but a deluge of nonstop world-class training had made him extremely effective at one thing, and one thing only: killing.

"Tangos neutralized. Proceeding to objective."

"Good kill. Good kill."

The team moved deeper into the base, encountering and neutralizing a few more armed personnel.

"Command, this is Ground Team. Approaching HVT location."

"Copy Red Six. Proceed with caution."

These Marines were *professionals*. The Ground Team breached an office door, finding three startled scientists sitting at a table: Viktor Kessler, Jessica Mercer, and Michael Walker.

In addition to their customary Laika KH-13 6.5 mm semi-automatic rifle that every Spectre carried as a primary weapon, each commando was armed with non-lethal stun guns. The non-lethal microwave emitter guns directed a focused beam of microwave energy at each target. Water molecules on the target's skin heated up rapidly, creating an intense burning sensation, but without causing lasting injury. It's quite literally microwaving their skin with hyper focused precision.

The three doctors froze in place, stupefied by the sudden interruption. As the three of the Spectres kept the stun guns focused on the HVTs, the other three threw thick bags over their heads and tightened them around their neck without causing suffocation. As they had practiced this drill several times over the past few days, the gunmen released the microwaves, allowing the Spectres to tie the terrorists hands behind their back.

Red Six signaled, "Ironbar, package secured."

"Green for exfil."

"Moving to extraction."

Cohen responded, "Acknowledged. Dustoff in three

Mikes." Cohen disengaged the intercom to the Ground Team and sent a separate encrypted message to the other operation.

The Marines escorted their three captives back to the docking bay. Another successful mission without any friendly casualties. Their starcraft's hatch cycled shut as the crew prepared for departure. The doctors' dinner was still steaming on the table.

Asher Cohen confirmed over the encrypted signal, "Stargazer, this is TALON Lead, objective complete, target secured."

"TALON has achieved objective. Withdraw APACHE. I repeat, withdraw APACHE," signaled through an encrypted line.

Captain Adam Harris stood at the command console with his crew. His Executive Officer gave a not-so-subtle fist bump but was reprimanded by his superior. "We're not out of the woods, yet."

Harris turned on the comm link to the Belter Naval Base and said, "Aristarkhov Command, this is UJF *McCarthy*. We are terminating exercises and withdrawing from the area. Over."

Sokolov turned to his XO, "Wait. They're actually pulling out?"

Sokolov keyed his mic.

"*McCarthy*, this is Aristarkhov Command. Confirm you are withdrawing. Over."

"Affirmative, Aristarkhov. We are ceasing all operations and departing." He then told them their ETA to leave international waters.

Sokolov instructed his staff to stand down and disengage all targeting systems. He signaled to Captain Harris, "Understood, *McCarthy*. We will monitor your withdrawal. Aristarkhov out."

Inside the UJF *McCarthy*, a radar operator signaled the Captain. "Sir, Belter fighters are breaking off. SAM systems powering down."

Harris said, "Let's get our boys home."

The destroyer cut a hard turn and burned hard back towards Jupiter, which appeared as nothing more than a bright red star. In the distance, two Belter starfighters banked and headed back to their base.

The purpose of war ain't killing. It's to get the other side to break morale and surrender. Each individual battle and skirmish is a step to this greater goal.

. . .

"Command, APACHE here. Calling in the dark. Mission accomplished. No casualties. TALON confirmed HVT capture. I repeat: TALON confirmed HVT capture. Moving to exfil."

"Excellent work, APACHE. By the time you get this, you're already headed our way. See you boys back at base."

The small command staff celebrated the victory with the usual jubilance, exclamations, jumps, and hugs.

Naomi Asimov, the Secretary of Defense, congratulated the crew. "Well done, everyone. Let's keep our eyes on the screens until they're safely home. Assholes and elbows."

27

DANIELLE FREEMAN AND ASHER COHEN SAT IN A BALCONY overlooking the President's slow and precise commencement address. He had just informed the nation that after the past few months of sporadic terrorist attacks, those who were primarily responsible had been apprehended. The speech was filled with adulation for the intelligence agency and for the armed forces' service. The next few months would be an onslaught of legal procedures and hearings to find out how this happened, how to prevent it from happening again, and how to best serve justice to those responsible.

"If they wanted to be effective and under the radar, why not just use gas and poison the life support system? Going through all this extra effort requires-"

Freeman interrupted Cohen, "You can't assume they think like normal Jovians. You're attempting to apply reason to terrorists. They're psychopaths."

"I'm just saying, there are a lot more *pragmatic* ways to accomplish their goal. I respect the work ethic, but it's fucked up."

"Yeah, well. Only Belters bleed."

Cohen let out a deep sigh. He mixed a cocktail and handed a glass to her. He told her to drink it.

"What is it?"

"It's called a Godfather. Alex got me into them a while back." Saying his name still stung him a little bit. This drink was not laced with anything sinister, it was just a good ol' fashioned Godfather cocktail.

Freeman raised her glass and said, "To a successful address."

"Yeah. He did well today."

The glasses clinked and they drank.

Freeman said, "You know, I never properly thanked you."

"Just doing my job, ma'am."

The Director leaned in with an arm around Cohen's shoulder and said, "No, it was more than that. What you did... she would be proud."

"Who?"

"Your wife."

He was no stranger to handshakes and high fives, but to be honest, he didn't remember the last time he received a hug from someone else. He shook the glass slightly to let the ice clink against one another. Staring at his drink, he said, "I hope so."

Humans never change. Not really. Individuals may, but as a

whole they do not. Wars come and go, but there it remains, our faithful companion. There is always war. The destruction that an idea can lead to. And so it goes. The cycle of war without end.

"Men like you, Cohen... the ones who work behind the scenes. You're the real heroes." She took another sip and turned away to the window.

"Heroes? We're just people doing what needs to be done."

AFTERWORD

Please leave an honest review for my book wherever you purchased it. I would appreciate it if you do this right now while it is still fresh in your memory.

I've been working on this novel, or perhaps it's a novella at this point, for about 18 months now. It truly has been a labor of love and something I find myself chipping away at everyday. Today is a bit bizarre for me as I just gutted about 100 pages from the story and my final draft is due for submission in four days. This story has gone upwards to 100,000 words to its current form under 45,000. As it ebbs and flows, the tone has really shifted to something more serious rather than earlier renditions which had more of an action/comedy feel to it.

My first draft in summer 2024 was about corporate espionage and a whistleblower. I wasn't enthusiastic about the story I was trying to tell. Believe it or not, Asher Cohen was originally written as a villain. I kept some of the characters and worldbuilding, and created a new story about terrorism and national security. This shift was after I had read seven Tom Clancy novels within 3 months. Shocker that I'm a Clancy fan, I know.

I wanted to create something that paid homage to my love of science fiction, our solar system, and the macho-man action films of the 1980's and 1990's that I grew up with. Oddly enough, I just watched a Rambo movie for the first time last week with First Blood (1982). I was expecting it to be a campy generic action film that was full of one-liners and explosions, but what I saw was an exposition on PTSD, crooked cops, and concise storytelling. From what I've read, the original cut for the movie was three hours long and Stallone hated it. He thought it would ruin his career and even offered to pay for the production costs so long as no one else saw it. It was truly terrible. In the original draft, whenever Rambo would be struck by a crooked cop, he would say some one-liner along the lines of "Is that all you got?" At one point he killed an owl and yelled, "Take that you mouse-munching motherfucker!" Peak cinema.

The director wanted to make it work so he took notes from Stallone on his next cut of the film, which would eventually become the theatrical version we know and love. They removed any scenes that didn't directly push the plot forward. Ninety minutes and only one confirmed death on screen. It's a tightly knit story that focuses on how one veteran going through a rough time was pushed into a corner until he started to fight back.

I wanted to keep this story as tightly knit as possible and tried my best to focus on good ol' fashioned storytelling. I appreciate you taking the time to read my story.

Thank you for reading!

Josef Kainrad

GLOSSARY

Astronomical Unit - A unit of measurement for 149,597,870.7 km. The average distance the Earth is from the Sun.

Atomics - Nuclear or atomic weaponry.

The Belt - The Belter Empire is a transplanetary country that spans much of the Asteroid Belt, including Ceres, Iris, and Vesta.

Callisto - The furthest of the Galilean moons of Jupiter.

The Castrum - The capitol building for Ganymede Republic.

Ceres - The largest dwarf planet in the Asteroid Belt. The capital state for the Belt. Discovered in 1801 by Giuseppe Piazzi. It was the first asteroid discovered. Ceres was considered to be a fully fledged planet until 1852 when the classification of what a planet is was narrowed.

CSS - The Committee for State Security is the international intelligence agency for the federal government of the Belter Empire. The organization operates as a military entity, adhering to army laws and regulations. Its responsibilities encompassed internal security, foreign intelligence, counter-intelligence, and secret police activities. It is headquartered on Ceres.

The Defense Intelligence Agency (DIA) - A civilian foreign intelligence agency for the federal government of the United Jovian System. Its official duties include collecting, processing, and analyzing global national security information, primarily using human intelligence, and carrying out covert operations through its Directorate of Operations. It is headquartered in Roosevelt.

Derry - The capital city for the Ganymede Republic. It is the home of the Castrum and the SIS headquarters.

Europa- One of the Galilean moons of Jupiter.

Extravehicular Activity Suit (EVA) - A space suit that is a specially designed garment worn by astronauts during spacewalks or extravehicular activities. It provides life support, protection from the harsh conditions of space, and mobility for astronauts working outside spacecraft or space stations. EVA suits typically include a helmet, gloves, life support system, and layers of material to shield astronauts from temperature extremes and micrometeoroids.

Galilean Moons - The moons of Jupiter discovered by Galileo Galilei: Io, Europa, Ganymede, and Callisto.

Gan De Station - A research facility located in the Southern hemisphere of Europa, operated by the United Jovian Europan Program, which falls under the jurisdiction of the UJS and is affiliated with the National Science Foundation. Gan De was a Chinese astronomer and scientist known for his meticulous observation of celestial bodies and his contributions to early astronomical knowledge in ancient China, particularly in the field of lunar and planetary observation.

Ganymede - The largest moon of Jupiter. Home to UJS and GR. Ganymede is one of the largest objects in the solar system. It is one of the only rocks orbiting our sun that has its own magnetic field produced by the convective motion of a liquid core that protects against cosmic radiation, solar radiation, and solar wind, called a magnetosphere. Ganymede is 778 million km (5.2 AU) from Sol. From Ganymede, Sol is 1/5 this size as it would be from Earth's horizon (roughly the size of a quarter held at arm's length). This would be about the size of a green pea in the sky. Not much more than a very bright star in the black canvas of the big empty. Occasionally the Earth appears as a pale blue dot in the Ganymedean horizon. Ganymede is made up of 23 districts with 11 metropolitan boroughs and 12 two-tier non-metropolitan districts. 18 districts which are governed by the UJS, including the capital district of Roosevelt.

Ganymede First (GF) - Ganymede First is a Ganymede Republic grassroots political movement that seeks to end UJS rule in Olympus, facilitate Ganymede unification and bring about an independent republic encompassing all of Western Ganymede.

Ganymede Republic Provisional Army (GRPA) - Originally a paramilitary force during the revolution, it is now the de facto armed forces branch for the Ganymede Republic. Although currently the only national defense for the Western districts, it does not report directly to the Ganymede Republic's legislative body.

Io -The closest of the Galilean moons to Jupiter.

Jovian - The original term referred to the Jovian System. Now it is a term relating to or characteristic of the UJS or its inhabitants.

Jovian National News (JNN) - A prominent national daily newspaper head-quartered in New London. Renowned as a newspaper of record, it stands as the second-largest newspaper by circulation and holds a place as one of the United Jovian System's longest running newspapers.

The Jovian System - Jupiter, its rings, and its moons.

Jupiter - The largest planet in our solar system. The Sun accounts for 99.8% of all mass in our solar system. Jupiter is around ⅔ of the remaining .2%, making up .13% of the net total mass in the solar system. Another way to phrase it would be: Jupiter makes up around 2/3 of all mass in our solar system when discounting the star we orbit. With a diameter of 142,800 km, it is eleven times bigger than Earth and thirteen-hundred times the volume. This means that you could fit 1300 Earths inside of Jupiter. In fact, Jupiter is so massive that it does not even orbit the Sun. The Sun and Jupiter both orbit a center of gravity betwixt one another called a barycenter. Their relationship differs as it is the only one with a barycenter outside the Sun. All the other kids in the neighborhood have their barycenter inside the star's mass. Mankind has always been able to see Jupiter with the naked eye. The discovery of her moons happened at the tail end of the Italian Renaissance. Galileo Galilei had a pivotal moment between 1609 and 1610, when he peered through the lens of his homemade telescope. What initially appeared to be three unassuming stars arranged in a linear dance that appeared to be orbiting Jupiter itself. Galileo had discovered it was actually four of Jupiter's largest moons: Ganymede, Europa, Callisto, and Io. They are known as the Galilean moons while the entire Jupiter and moon complex is the Jovian System.

Hilda 153 - An object in the Asteroid Belt that orbits throughout the outer-most layer.

Intelligence and Security Command (INSCOM) - A direct reporting unit of the UJS Armed Forces, specializing in intelligence, security, and informa-tion operations for UJS commanders, collaborators in the Intelligence Community, and national decision-makers. INSCOM is centrally located at Fort Bradbury, outside of Roosevelt, Ganymede.

Iris - An asteroid in the Asteroid Belt.

Laika, Inc - A private weapons manufacturing enterprise in the Belt dedicated to design, manufacturing, and marketing firearms for law enforcement, military, and commercial use. Laika was the first dog in space.

Luna - Earth's sole moon, commonly known as 'The Moon.' Luna is Latin for 'moon.'

North Callisto - An independent protectorate country. It is under the protection of the UJS for defense while maintaining autonomy over domestic affairs.

Orbital Patrol - A branch of the UJS armed forces. It is under the jurisdiction of the Department of Transportation and is responsible for the protection of life and property in orbit in the Jovian System.

Rear Echelon Motherfucker (REMF) - A slang term to refer to individuals who are perceived to be stationed or working in non-combat roles, away from the front lines.

Rockwell Corporation - A weapons manufacturer based in orbit around Jupiter. Rockwell Corporation is a publicly traded aerospace and defense company. It is the fifth-largest defense contractor based on arms sales. Alphonso David Rockwell was important for his significant contributions to the field of aerospace engineering, particularly for his work on the development of the Apollo lunar module. His expertise played a crucial role in the success of NASA's Apollo program, including the historic Apollo II mission that landed the first humans on Luna.

Roosevelt - The capital city for UJS and home to the DIA headquarters.

Special Intelligence Service (SIS) - The intelligence agency for the federal government of the Ganymede Republic. The unit specializes in various domestic and international roles, including counter-terrorism, hostage rescue, direct action, and covert reconnaissance. A significant amount of information about the SIS is classified, and neither the Ganymede Republic government nor the Department of Defense comments on the unit due to the secrecy and sensitivity of its operations. It is headquartered in Derry.

Spectre - A special operations group for the UJS Marine Corps. They are known for their expertise in special reconnaissance, counter-terrorism, and unconventional warfare.

The Spectre Training Program (SPECTRAP) - A rigorous selection process characterized by its high dropout rate of 95%. This program is meticulously structured to sift out individuals unable to fulfill its rigorous physical and mental prerequisites, resulting in a significant attrition rate. Fatalities have been documented during the course of SPECTRAP due to the extreme intensity of the training exercises.

Tereshkova - A spacecraft manufacturer, launch service provider, defense contractor, and satellite communications specialist. Valentina Tereshkova was the first woman in space.

Transit Rail System (TRAS) - A high-speed magnetic levitation railway connecting the districts of Ganymede.

Tycho UJS - A non-governmental Jovian enterprise specializing in the creation, production, and promotion of firearms catering to law enforcement, military, and commercial sectors. Tycho Brahe was a Renaissance-era Danish astronomer renowned for his meticulous and remarkably precise astronomical observations before the invention of the telescope.

The United Jovian System (UJS) - A transplanetary country primarily located in Ganymede, Callisto, Io and Europa.

Vanguard Solutions - An American private defense manufacturer with global interests specializing in aerospace, arms, defense, information security, medicinal, and technology sectors.

Verdeguay - A small nation on Callisto.

Vesta - The brightest asteroid visible from Earth. It is an asteroid in the Asteroid Belt. Vesta has the largest mountain known in the Solar System.

ABOUT THE AUTHOR

Josef Kainrad currently lives in Portland, Oregon with his fiancee and two larger-than-life dogs.

Terminal Velocity is his first novel.

Made in the USA
Monee, IL
30 December 2024

72529885R00125